Silhouettes of Time

short stories
by

Maya Mitra Das

Azalea Art Press
Southern Pines . North Carolina

ISBN: 978-1-943471-07-2

The Harvest Moon
by Maya Mitra Das

Summer was shy
To say goodbye
The harvest moon was up
Filling the sky

The trees swayed
In the gentle breeze
Murmuring their songs
To a misty dream

The moon like a
Baked round loaf
Peeped through the
Drifting clouds

Over the moonstruck land
Along with hoot of owls
I traveled back in time
To a far away place

Landing
On a moon-brushed house
In an old, familiar courtyard
Yes here! Yes here!

Under the harvest moon
I played and danced
I danced and played
With my loving Grandmother

All the way
until the dawn

Dedication:

I dedicate my book to my father, the late Dr. Sailendra Prosad Mitra.

Whenever we had time to talk, he would give me ideas about music, art, history, archeology and many other subjects. His constant, patient teachings inspired me to pursue interests besides my profession in medicine.

I do not know whether I fulfilled his expectations, but because of his guidance and inspiration I am who I am now.

CONTENTS

Foreword

❧

When Maya Mitra Das walked into my creative writing class nearly six years ago, I knew she was special.

She promptly informed me that, for a "woman of a certain age," she was not only a medical doctor but also actively performing classical Indian dances, playing piano monthly with her fellow pianists and taking poetry classes through a local adult education course. Then, I thought, *How in the world is she going fit creative writing into all of this?*

I proceeded to tell her that while creative writing can be approached in a relaxed manner, it's not an activity that one should treat as a passing fancy. Students in my creative writing classes have learned the serious craft of this fine literary art, paying homage to great literary artists that have blazed the trail before us, but we have also surrendered to that fun, whimsical part of ourselves.

Maya has learned to be both scholar and artist. Despite her earlier reservations of not having had any creative writing experience, Maya has blossomed into a true creative spirit. She has embraced what it means to be a literary artist in every sense of the word as her stories transcend realms of time, space and memory. Evidence of her artistry and versatility has resulted in the birth of the book you now hold in your hands.

Sit back and relax as you are transported back and forth in time to familiar locales and exotic landscapes. Allow yourself to be lulled into a dreamscape by Maya's lyrical prose, akin to a beloved lullaby as her words both soothe and entertain you through her characters who are as colorful as the saris worn by the women in her stories and as textural as the artistic and spiritual canvas that is her native India and beyond.

It has been my honor not only to have Maya in my class but also to have served as her "literary guru," as she has endeavored to present to you her wonderful tapestry of stories straight from her heart.

– *Janice De Jesus*
Creative Writing Instructor
January, 2016

Silhouettes of Time

Manjari and the Ballad of Peace

The sun sank slowly beyond the horizon as the last glow of the day flooded the fields and the valleys. The tall *Shaal* and *Pyall* trees started to move their limbs with the gentle breeze. The *Sonajhuri* trees began to murmur their tune greeting the birds in their nests. The chirping of the birds filled the air, welcoming the evening.

After a long exhausting day at work, Manjari started strumming her *sharod*, sitting comfortably on a padded bench on her patio. She sat close to a tree with branches full of big red flowers. Growing upwards, they looked like the flames of a fire. Her long wavy black hair covered her arms.

The black clouds on the horizon appeared suddenly, and the wind came up, blowing Manjari's hair and exposing her sculpted arms. Her olive-colored skin looked brighter with the flash of lightning. Standing five-feet-three inches tall, Manjari's slim figure complimented her skin, her pointed nose and wide, black eyes that were melancholic. Her colorful sari, adorned with ostentatious jewelry, only enhanced her beauty. Manjari carried a mysterious air about her—not quite reserved, but guarded somehow. Only when someone was able to crack through her emotional shell was she able to show her relaxed nature.

Manjari lived in a small bungalow one hundred fifty kilometers from Kolkata, India. The year was 1972. She taught history at a nearby college in town. Her *sharod* was the only precious possession she had saved from her past. The lightning and thunder continued to dominate the sky and with it Manjari's memories flashed. In her mind's eye, she could see the small village where she was born and where she had lived with her parents.

The village was on the other side of river Padma in the east side of undivided Bengal. Fond memories of her school and her friends passed by one by one like drifting clouds.

Lush green paddy fields and coconut trees bordered the village, and beyond that a railway threaded through the field. The trains whizzed by, whistling with the wind. A big pond occupied space near Manjari's home. It used to be full of clear blue water and blossoming pink lotuses during the autumn. This pond also supplied edible fish all year round.

The evenings, Manjari remembered, were spectacular—filled with clear starry skies, gentle breezes, chirping crickets, and dancing fireflies beyond the house around the paddy fields. As the evening drew its curtain, separating day from night, the frogs would begin their serenade and Manjari's eyelids would grow heavy until she fell asleep.

These were the days when people around the village exchanged niceties and seemed to trust each other. As the adults came home from a long day's work, children would settle in for the evening, busy preparing their homework for next day.

It was a very peaceful village existence that remained that way for many years.

Then one day in 1946, the life that young Manjari grew to love changed forever. An unrelenting, uneasy aura of secrecy that the nine-year-old didn't understand infiltrated the air.

One night Manjari's parents came and sat down next to her as she did her homework. Her mother, Bakul, fondly arranged her curly bangs as her father, Bipin, addressed her by her pet name.

"Manju, we need to talk before you go to bed."

"Yes, daddy?"

"Manju, you probably noticed that some neighbors aren't so friendly anymore and have avoided us."

Manjari shrugged. "I noticed but don't know why. Did we do something wrong to make them angry?"

Her parents shook their heads sadly.

"You must know that there's religious unrest between Hindus and Muslims and it's escalating," Bipin said. "There was a time in this part of the country that there were temples and mosques around the villages and people practiced their own religious rites without question and celebrated each others' festivities. They are not happy right now with this arrangement and do not want to live peacefully, side by side together as we have done for so many years. The people are so angry at each other that they are destroying and looting things from the people who are not of the same religious belief as they are. Some groups are killing each other. The part of India where we are, and the extreme west side of India like Lahore and west side of Punjab, are very much affected."

"What are you talking about? People killing people of the same country? Does it mean that I am not going to be friends with Fatima and Sayeeda?"

"You will be always their friend," her father assured her. "All I'm saying is that if we have to risk our lives to live here then we have to move to a safer area, like a hundred kilometers away from the big city Kolkata. And I can take a teaching job there for the time being; until the situation improves."

"Mahjusona don't tell anyone, we have to leave our home secretly, so that no one knows," Bakul said. "Do you understand?"

Manjari felt confused and frightened. "No, I won't tell anyone. I promise."

Disillusioned by the way people were slaughtering each other, Manjari realized that one of her friends, Champa, had already left. It felt strange that Champa did not say goodbye to her. Champa's house and rice granary had been on fire. It was not an accident, was it? Manjari realized that her father was right. Someone not to be trusted must have done harm to them.

The couple planned to leave their home with Manjari during a New Moon evening when an escape in the dark seemed more feasible. Then the day of their escape finally arrived; that ominous day when a peaceful evening settled with a hoot of an owl, soon interrupted by an unpleasant bang on the door followed by several loud voices coming from the front door.

"Who is it?" Bipin said. His voice dripped with fear.

Before he could open the door, the people stampeded their way through the door, dismantling and destroying the furniture and looting possessions on their destructive path.

Manjari, pale with fear and anxiety, ran to her mother Bakul and started sobbing. She grabbed her tightly with her two hands.

Bipin attempted to reason with the intruders whom he knew from school where he was the principal.

"Yusuf and Kareem you were my beloved students! What is wrong? Why are you doing this?"

"Why do you ask?" Yusuf snarled.

"You will find out soon."

Bipin and Yusuf wrestled. As Bipin tried to defend him, Kareem took out his sharp knife and plunged it into Bipin's chest who fell with a loud cry in a pool of his own blood.

"We have to transport these two to Mr. Khan's house," Kareem said. "Before that we can play around a little with these women. The girl is too young. We can wait till she matures."

Bakul, who heard the conversation, ran out to the kitchen only to succumb to the same sharp knife that took her husband's life. Soon Bipin's and Bakul's blood combined into one large, tragic pool. Just a few feet away stood Manjari in shock from what she had witnessed.

Please, let this just be a nightmare. Let it not be true, she pleaded silently.

Kareem pushed her down and tied her feet and both hands. They blindfolded her and threatened to torture her if she made noise. As they lifted her, she could imagine seeing her parents' pale faces for one last time. Even death couldn't erase a somewhat serene countenance as they passed from this dreadful world. She could remember the look on their faces as her kidnappers shoved her into a horse-drawn buggy that made a hasty escape. She could see the sky in her imagination as clear and starry as wind blew gently over her face. She truly believed that the fireflies danced madly around the paddy fields. Peace existed amid the smell of death.

Meanwhile, in Noyakhali, the east part of Bengal, about twenty-five miles east of Manjari's tortured home, the scene at Mahatma Gandhi's Peace Camp was bustling as people occupied themselves with plans for a mission of liberation. Gandhi's followers fondly called him *"Bapujee"* —a name known by people all over India who regarded him as a father figure. Arun, who was a notable activist and instrumental in starting the camp, came forward and said, *"Bapujee,* Bivajee has arrived."

Arun had been arrested by the British government, as he was actively involved in the revolution against the British. He was imprisoned for four years. After he was released, he entered this part of the country disguised as a

Muslim orthodox cleric, as it was almost impossible to get in when the communal riot was at its peak. Arun was brave enough to start the Peace Camp alone to serve the distressed people who lost everything including loved ones in this sad, communal riot—and also to serve the children who lost their parents. After he established the Peace Camp, Mahatma Gandhi was notified, and he came to visit the camp himself and was pleased. It was in the news that "a Peace Camp exists in the east part of Bengal."

Biva, a recent graduate of Calcutta University, was a writer and vocalist in Indian classical music and took an active role with her physician husband in the underground work against British rule. She could not take the deception of living sheltered in the family when the rest of the country was in serious trouble.

Standing at five-feet-two inches tall, with a healthy smooth tanned complexion, Biva's triangular face held a prominent nose and beautiful wide, bright eyes, which sparkled. She tucked her long, wavy hair in a bun, which complimented her conservative attire. She was known to command an arresting presence everywhere she went.

The followers listened in awe as Gandhi discussed the various missions, many of them arduous and risky. He informed the camp that some girls had been kidnapped after their parents were murdered. For ten abducted girls people knew the places where they were taken. Negotiations would be offered for their freedom. But one girl, the daughter of a prominent school headmaster, whose whereabouts was unknown, captivated Biva's attention. She came forward and volunteered that she would take on the task of finding one of the missing girls—Manjari. Mahatma Gandhi expressed that the mission was risky but praised Biva for her bravery. After the discussion, Gandhi started his morning walk attired in his signature white outfit, firmly holding his long stick. With his followers in tow, they started singing a *Tagore* song loudly together:

> *If no one responds to your call, then you just march alone, on your own, on your own—keep going on your own. If no one shines light, Oh, poor Hapless soul—If they shut the doors of their homes, on a dark tempestuous night, then in the fire of lightning and thunder—Let the ribs of your chest be alight—And burn, burn alone!*

The peace march continued every morning for at least two hours. The march wound around the muddy unpaved road as their voices echoed through the swaying paddy fields and beyond. A train charged by at a distance beyond the tall coconut trees. The people around the villages anxiously looked through the window wondering what was going on.

"What is the purpose of this peace march?" some brave souls inquired.

"To let you know that we are here for you and with you. You are not alone," a peace marcher responded.

"Can you stop this? What role can we play in this mission?" a villager asked.

"I am not going to quit until I come to an agreement, and for you my advice would be to stand courageously together and confront the senseless communal riot between Hindus and Muslims," Gandhi replied.

After the peace march, they came and began their sessions at a spinning wheel to spin yarn of their own to make their own clothes. Gandhi believed that if you could make your own yarn, and weave your own clothes, it would make you independent of buying clothes made in England.

The Peace Camp ran like a moderate-sized institution. There was a big kitchen where food was being prepared three times daily for distressed people who took shelter with the children, the children who had lost their parents and the people who were running the camp. A facility existed for the children to study and play and enjoy other activities to keep them busy. Gandhi made it clear that everything should be spotlessly clean around the camp and the adults who took refuge were given the responsibility all day long. There were two or three doctors on duty to deal with the ailments of the distressed people and children. At the end of the day there was a prayer meeting with devotional songs. One song said: "Almighty, please show us the path of peace, and bless us with the wisdom of peace. God or Almighty is the same one, with a different name Allah or Ishwar," and was followed by a discussion session. The day would end with the orange glow of the sun over the swaying paddy fields. The cool gentle breeze blew through the palm trees as the evening settled.

❀❀❀

Manjari was transported by horse-drawn buggy to Mr. Khan's place. Once they reached their destination, Manjari, still numb with shock, did not know where they had taken her. She looked around in the dark but could not see. The people who murdered her parents dragged her inside, and then she placed her weary head to rest on the floor. When she woke up she realized she must have been asleep for hours. Had the recent events been a nightmare? She realized the trauma actually happened. She tried to lift her head up, and saw some shadowy figure.

"Time to get up!" Manjari heard someone say.

Wearily she felt her cold feet and fingers tremble. She shuddered as she felt her nerves climb from her feet to her heart. Anxiety overcame her as a woman asked her name.

"Forget about that name," the woman curtly replied. "From now on you will be called Salatun."

Manjari kept quiet and did not want to confront her as she was actually overwhelmed by the fear of the unknown.

"Today I let you sleep late," the woman said. "Starting tomorrow you get up early and start your work of cleaning the entire house. You start cleaning downstairs, polish the furniture and Mashuma will let you know when you can go upstairs and start cleaning there. Mashuma is in charge of the kitchen where you're expected to help her. There are rules and regulations of the house, and you are going to listen to whatever she tells you to do. That is my order. Mashuma, show her where she will stay and give her some clothes and that black *burka* she'll always have to wear."

Mashuma seems about my mother's age, Manjari thought. She was of average build and had wheat-colored skin. Her face was triangular with big black eyes that appeared kind. Mashuma's long black hair was pulled tightly in a bun. Over her white sari the black *burka* covered her body except her head and face.

"Salatun, please follow me," Mashuma softly uttered.

Manjari felt like crying out loud at the sound of her newly-given name, but her throat was choking with fear and anxiety. She followed Mashuma to listen to the first of many orientations of this big mansion with many corridors and dark menacing corners. During this reluctant weary tour of the dungeon-like mansion, she realized how modest and tiny their cottage was, but it was nurtured with lots of love and affection. Looking back now, she knew that life with her parents could never be possible again.

Mashuma took Manjari to the end of the mansion and showed her the sleeping quarters. She told Manjari that the day started early—around five in the morning.

Then she went over a litany of arduous physically and mentally demanding household tasks such as cleaning all the rooms and corridors, both upstairs and downstairs, and tidying them up, and polishing the furniture. Manjari was forced to help prepare lunch and dinner. She was forbidden to go upstairs alone to clean the rooms and was always accompanied by Mashuma. As weary Manjari began to sob, Mashuma gave her a pat on the back and assured her she would help her.

Manjari toiled through the same routine orchestrated by the woman of the house and supervised by Mashuma. At times Manjari would encounter Sameema and her husband, Mr. Khan.

"Salatun, you did a sloppy job of tidying my bed," Sameema complained. "The bedspread should be changed every three days. I cannot stand to sleep in squalor and the mirror of my dresser has streaks. Next time I expect better than this."

It seemed to Manjari, that no matter how hard she tried, Sameema was never pleased.

So the unbearable days lingered on with only one relief—Mashuma's compassionate face and helping hand. At the risk of suffering from Sameema's wrath, Mashuma assisted in completing Manjari's household chores; including cleaning the obscenely large mirrors and dusting the framed photos of the Khan family. As she prepared the family's meals, Mashuma would encourage Manjari to take a break and engage her in conversation while still being on her guard, lest a family member barge in unexpectedly.

"This afternoon, the family will be gone to attend an event and are not expected to return till late evening," Mashuma said one day. "So I will take you out in the garden and we will chat to our heart's content. Finish the work quickly."

Manjari could not remember the last time she had been outdoors. Had it been months? A year?

While Manjari's heart was heavy with grief, the very idea of going outside made her eyes curious to see beyond the window. Manjari's mood briefly lifted as she stepped into the garden.

"I feel that I could breathe the fresh air, and I am so glad to smell the jasmine and tuberoses," Manjari said.

The gardenias were there in a medium-sized tree. She wanted to pluck one but, but knowing that she was forbidden to do so, she avoided the temptation to make contact with the flower.

Suddenly, memories of Manjari's once blissful home, with its pond and garden once lovingly tended by her mother, flooded her consciousness. She sunk her head and grieving heart and curled into a ball as she surrendered to tears. Mashuma came and patted her softly on the back.

Mashuma sighed as she shared her own tragic tale.

"You know, Salatun, I am also not Muslim. My name was changed, as these people would have killed us. In exchange, I begged them to save me and my husband's life, and I promised to serve them as long as they needed me."

Manjari waited until Mashuma continued her story.

"Our whole family—my parents and my child—planned to escape in two different delivery trucks of fruit and vegetables. But we got caught," Mashuma said.

"Do you know anything about your parents and daughter?" Manjari gently asked.

"Yes, that they are safe and alive residing at the outskirt of the big city Kolkata. But, my husband . . ." Mashuma paused, realizing she'd said too much. "That is all for today."

The black clouds gathered on the eastern side of the horizon as a blast of cool breeze blew through the trees. They heard a chorus of some sort that sounded like prayer songs from a distance.

"That is from the Peace Camp of Mahatma Gandhi. It is on other side of the river," Mashuma told Manjari. "You see, the river is beyond that paddy field and the Peace Camp is farther away from the river bank. The Peace Camp is a place where the distressed people—victims of this senseless riot—can take refuge. I heard of it when we were planning to escape; it was the talk of the town and there were posters plastered in places like the vegetable and fish markets."

Manjari's memories of the last few days of peaceful existence with her parents came back to her. She remembered her father mentioning the name of Mahatma Gandhi and that Gandhi and his fellow volunteers had arrived about twenty-five miles from where they used to live. Manjari could hear the echo of his father's voice. It seemed so real to her: *You know the Peace Camp was started by a young spirited person recently released from prison. He was arrested for the activities of revolution against the British. There are two ladies involved also in this endeavor.*

Manjari remembered her father's words as tears rolled down her cheeks. She felt that the whole world was crashing in front of her, and she was just floating with her tied up hands and feet on an endless ocean of pain. She wished she could be at the Peace Camp now or join her parents in Heaven.

The weather changed abruptly, matching Manjari's mood, and it seemed that there was the possibility of rain, followed by lightning. The birds flew with agonizing chatter from one branch to the other, warning each other of imminent danger.

Mashuma started collecting the mangoes, which the wind had blown from the trees, and started putting those in a basket. Then she and Manjari rushed back into the house.

If life was like the weather, Manjari thought, then she longed for the calm after the storm.

At Gandhi's Peace Camp, special events were shaping up. One of them was Biva's quest for Manjari.

"Why are you so eager to find this girl Manjari?" one of the volunteers dared to ask Biva.

"Somebody has to take the risk of finding this girl," Biva boldly answered. "What happens if we abandon her? It would be cruel to not even try to save her."

Biva's Grandmother once organized a protest with the women-folk to burn clothes made in England. As Indian-made clothes were banned, they had to suffer the wrath of the British Police and were arrested for civil disobedience. She also shared the stories of two young, educated women who risked their lives for the freedom of the country, and that she must have inherited her courage from her Grandmother and father, both of whom served time in jail for fighting for freedom.

"Someone there who worked for the British authority planted a rifle in our backyard at night without our knowledge and accused my father of treachery," Biva explained passionately. "He was thrown in jail and tortured and all his hard-earned money as a school teacher was frozen by the British government to punish him. Fighting for freedom is in my blood. So I am determined to do my part to save this girl!"

At the Peace Camp, Arun, the director, strategized Biva's mission including choosing Dhiren, a guide familiar with the region, to accompany her. As the day of the rescue drew near, Biva focused on what lay ahead and, as possible obstacles invaded her thoughts, she tried to remain optimistic. Her worst fear was not finding Manjari. Biva thought about her husband's support, as he allowed her to pursue this important mission. Faces of her loved ones—her mother, father, Grandmother, brothers and sisters—flashed in front of her as a sign that Biva had every reason to return home alive.

Then there was the plan to end one's life with respect—with honor and tradition—should the mission go awry.

Biva kept her cyanide package protected; nobody knew where she kept it. She planned to use it in a worst-case scenario, when she definitely would know that her honor was at stake. Arun knew her plan, so he instructed Dhiren to keep an eye on her as much as possible and under no circumstances was he to let her use the deadly poison as she might not be able to assess the situation and take the cyanide when it was not necessary. Arun gave this instruction to Dhiren: if he thought that Biva would be in real danger at the hand of the perpetrators and her honor would be at stake, Dhiren would behead Biva with a big sword and kill himself as well. Biva was not aware of this plan and neither was Gandhi. Gandhi expressed great concern over the mission to rescue Manjari, as this was the most dangerous mission of all.

Biva and Dhiren began their search for Manjari that day and continued for a week. The grueling search went on as they had to make up a different excuse each time to gain access inside homes when they visited local landlords. Sometimes they talked about the Peace Camp and invited them to visit Gandhi. Other times they discussed some road improvement project. They were getting frustrated with their search, as they didn't seem to be getting anywhere.

They were given the confidential information that a now ten-year-old abducted girl was held prisoner in a mansion of a rich landlord. So their target was to take a chance to investigate a few more rich landlords' mansions on the other side of river.

So the search for Manjari continued. The evening was peaceful and spectacular. The sky greeted them with stars, while the earth gifted them with a gentle breeze and wild fireflies.

From one side of the river stretched a unique bridge consisting of two bamboo planks, which lay horizontally side by side and tied together. The end of either side was fortified with strong vertical bamboo poles. As Biva clutched a covered lantern close to her body, she found that crossing the river in pitch darkness became a real gymnastic maneuver, so Biva advised her attendant to swim and wait for her on the other side of river.

When she arrived at the gate of the huge mansion she told the gatekeeper that she wanted to talk to the lady of the house. The gatekeeper was hesitant, but with Biva's persistent request, he finally granted her permission. Sameema, accompanied by Mashuma, greeted Biva, who explained that she and her other companions were touring this area to see if anyone was interested in volunteering their time to help build roads or help get electricity and safe, accessible drinking water.

"Are you interested in becoming involved in this project?' Biva asked.

Sameema seemed honored as she was never asked and given a chance to take an important role outside her household, so she invited the guests inside the house. Mashuma suddenly excused herself saying she wanted to check on something. In the meantime, Sameema left to find her attendant to make some tea and snacks.

At that very moment Manjari appeared to dust the photos and rosewood chairs in the long corridor. She was curious about the visitors and hoped they would notice her presence.

Biva's radar targeted the young girl immediately. It was Manjari.

"Did someone bring you here?" Biva whispered as she grabbed the girl's hand. "Manjari? Is it you?"

Manjari suppressed a sob as she heard her name.

"I've come to rescue you," Biva whispered.

"But, I do not know you," Manjari protested. "Are you really going to help?"

"There is no time to discuss," Biva replied anxiously. "You must trust me. There is no other way for you to get out from this place. Show me a window or open space from where we can try to get out."

With a strong sense she could trust this woman, Manjari quickly guided Biva to a small bathroom with an open window. They had to step onto a toilet to climb out of the room. Then, after Biva jumped out, she urged Manjari to jump into her arms.

"Don't worry. I'll catch you," Biva assured her. "You can trust me."

Manjari closed her eyes. This was it. Her ticket to freedom. She would risk escaping with this stranger or stay and die. Manjari surrendered into Biva's waiting arms. Relief soared through both their hearts. But they both ran as fast as they could. It was too early to celebrate. They had to run for their lives.

Covered with the same black *burka* Manjari wore, they blended into the darkness. Biva knew they needed to reach the bank of the river soon, but the shrubs and darkness made the path almost unbearable. They heard some noise and could see some semblance of roving lights near the mansion from a distance. They hurried their pace, tripping over branches, as they knew pursuers were on their way. At last they reached the bank of the river where Biva's attendant Dhiren was waiting. He helped them descend into the river and told them to swim under the water as long as they could and momentarily lift their heads up to catch their breaths. Every moment was filled with uncertainty as they swam in the darkness. Manjari was glad that her father had taught her one of the greatest gifts of life—how to swim. Now, she wasn't just swimming to save her life. She was swimming to honor her parents.

They swam to the safe side of the river and finally reached the shore of the Peace Camp. As they reached the camp, the guard dogs started barking with excitement. The Peace Camp was barbed-wired all around, and there were armed guards with swords and bamboos. Guards posted themselves at each of the four corners of the camp.

They were specially trained to defend and fight in any emergency, and Arun demanded that the guards serve vigilant eight-hour shifts. Suddenly, the Peace Camp erupted into peals of relief and jubilation as they greeted the long-awaited arrivals, who were laden with mud and exhaustion but lucky to be alive.

The next few surreal hours passed as Manjari realized that she was no longer in danger. On the way to the Peace Camp, they heard the continuous serenade of crickets and croaking of frogs. Their vision turned over the paddy fields where the fireflies were dancing madly. Freedom was hers.

Manjari couldn't sleep that night. She kept thinking this was all a dream—that she was really still back at the mansion with that horrible Sameema's barking orders. Then gradually, she absorbed the ambience of the place her father mentioned at a time that seemed like ages ago. There were other young children in the camp, a few accompanied by their parents, while others lost their fathers, and some were totally orphaned like her. Day after day, she adjusted to life at the camp. Manjari continued to trust Biva—after all, the woman risked her own life to save hers. Trust turned into gratitude and gratitude turned into love. What choice did Manjari have but to choose love—which always conquered fear, her mother had told her. In time, Biva would become a surrogate mother to Manjari.

Then one day, Manjari received an unforgettable invitation—a chance to meet Gandhi.

"He is very kind and he loves all the children very much," Biva assured her.

When Mahatma Gandhi arrived, everyone in the camp seemed to be in collective awe in his presence. The children gathered round, waiting to be hugged by the great leader as though he was their Grandfather—the Father of all Fathers.

"I prayed for my Dad," said one little boy whose father was murdered.

"I pray for your long healthy and happy life," Gandhi told the boy.

Biva introduced Manjari to Gandhi who seemed very pleased to see them.

"With God's grace I am happy to see you alive and healthy," he said. "Biva, I am so happy to see you, and I am very proud that you fulfilled your task with courage and determination."

He turned to Manjari. "Manjari, my child, come here. Biva risked her life to save you. Always know that your parents are in a more peaceful place, and they are constantly watching over you."

Manjari was in tears as she hugged Biva. This was the first time she showed her intense emotion to Biva. Gandhijee ushered Biva and Manjari to a room where a mat made of knitted palm leaves was spread across the floor. There were a few pillows with embroidered covers laid on the mat at the corner, and a large clay vase with tuberoses. A large spinning wheel sat in the middle of room waiting to be spun.

"I heard you did very well in school," Gandhi told Manjari. "Do you want to continue your studies?"

"How? My parents are no more," Manjari wondered as tears began to well in her eyes.

"We know your situation," Gandhi said. "Suppose we arranged for it?"

Manjari expressed her concern over not knowing where she would live. Gandhi assured her that volunteers had raised funds to open a new school with a dormitory for the girls set to open soon around the city of Kolkata.

"You will go there and continue your education," he said. "You have to do it for yourself and for your parents to survive in this world. Biva will look after you and guide you whenever you need her."

Manjari was overwhelmed with joy and simultaneous fear of the unknown. Despite her tears Manjari raised a smile of gratitude to Biva, who returned her smile. In the background, the singing vibrated all over Peace Camp. They were singing:

If everyone goes back / Oh you poor hapless soul / While you walk on the desolate road, no one looks back / Then just move on, trampling the thorns on the road under your bloodied feet / All on your own

India got independence and the country was divided. Manjari attended boarding school with Biva as a mentor. She gradually overcame her emotional hurdles that outweighed her academic challenge. She slowly learned to adjust and regain control over her traumas with

Biva's guidance and support as the years went by. Even as Biva had children of her own, she was always there to see Manjari achieve important personal and educational goals.

Years later, as head of the history department in a university one hundred and fifty kilometers from Kolkata, Manjari thought about how to make history come alive to her students. She smiled peacefully as she decided she would share with her students and with future generations her own tale, her parent's tale and her country's story of love, pain, survival and freedom.

As the evening settled in slowly, the smell of the exotic *Mohua* flower wafted through the air just as the red moon peeped through the distant mountain range. Manjari could hear the beating of *Madal* percussion drums as the tribes danced and sang along with the gentle breeze. Manjari closed her eyes as she embraced the memories— both good and bad—of her village, parents, her slavery in that mansion, Biva, and the Peace Camp. The song rang eternally in her head:

> *If all of them turn their faces, feeling scared, one and all, then just open your heart . . . This is the ballad of peace, love and freedom for all.*

A Lily Blooms in Summer

In the summer of 1950, Lily sat relaxing in her Tudor revival-style house in Charleston, South Carolina, her lifelong home, reminiscing about the years since she was in high school.

The tall living room windows invited the lights, sounds and scents of the outdoors. A sweet, lemony candy-like smell filled the air. As she gazed outside, the blooming magnolias swayed by a gentle breeze near the door making her drowsy.

In the living room, over the mantel, there was a painting of Rome and a portrait of Lily as a young girl. In this living room, she had danced with music provided by a rented jukebox to songs that included "I'm Gonna Meet my Sweetie Now," by Jean Goldkette and his orchestra; "Back in your Own Backyard," by Paul Whitman; and "Because My Baby Do Not Mean Maybe," by Frank Frey and George Wilson. As Lily sat on her floral sofa, she felt herself being transported into the past.

In 1925, when Lily was in high school, she was full of life and ready to explore the world. Though she led a life full of activities and fun, she was still sheltered. The girls in her class were up to something. They wanted to break away from their parents' way of conservative living and do something fun. They wanted a night out that included a dance party and young men to dance with. It was an ideal concept, but how to materialize the idea was a challenge.

She sent a message to her cousin on her mother's side, who was a graduate student at the University of South Carolina:

> Dear Doug,
> I want to meet with you and discuss a very serious matter. Please let me know where we can meet. I prefer we meet elsewhere, not in our house. Looking forward to your response.
> All the best, Lily

Lily's mother, Betsy, was very close to her sister, Nelly, who used to live in Charleston not far from Betsy. Doug used to come regularly to spend time with Lily in her house with his mother when his father was out on a business trip. Doug, who was four years older than Lily, was very protective of her.

When Doug found out about Lily's desire to attend a dance party, he was very reluctant; but with Lily's insistence he agreed at last. In roaring 1925, she arranged a dance party with cousin Doug's blessing and careful planning.

Doug selected his friends from the University of South Carolina to be guests at the party. He looked into different locations in Charleston, but selected a clubhouse near the university, close to the river. The promenade served as a lovely site for walking in the evening and spending leisure time. The clubhouse was surrounded by a beautiful lawn with tall trees and decorative shrubs. Inside the clubhouse, the main hall featured a wooden dance floor and a moderate-sized stage.

The young men assembled in the clubhouse on a lovely summer evening as the sun was descending to the west, but the sky was bright and glowing.

The girls, wearing their flappers' dresses and high heels entered slowly; some arriving with long gloves, hats, necklaces and other accessories, and some with a sparkling band across the forehead with a peacock feather. Lily dressed in a black below-the-knee flapper dress and several long pearl necklaces, which dangled rhythmically as she entered the clubhouse. Lily's light-colored skin glowed in the dusk.

They mingled and somewhat got acquainted with each other when Lily's cousin, dressed in a tux, stood on the bandstand announced, "Thank you all for coming. Warren, my friend from Princeton, is equally talented in math and physics; but today, he will show off his expertise with the violin."

Warren stood tall, an olive-skinned figure with big bright black eyes shining like two glowing candles in the dark night. Warren sported a navy double-breasted suit and a pocket watch, attracting not just Lily's attention—other ladies stood poised nearby, subtly arranging their coiffed hairstyles and vying for Warren's attention.

As Warren started playing his violin, the audience was mesmerized. There was a joyous roar along with an ovation after he finished his piece.

Lily was spellbound. As all the girls circled around Warren, Lily stood a few feet away, casting her lovely brown eyes on him. She was sure that her apparent distance from the ogling girls would make her stand out in the crowd.

Once the music and dancing began, Warren sauntered towards her. Her heart and pulse pulsated rapidly as he stood in front of her, his hand extended. As she allowed her slender frame to surrender to his capable arms and confident lead, Lily soon realized that Warren was a very good dancer. She wanted to give herself completely and wished that they would dance forever— that time would stand still. After a few dances, Lily hinted that she longed to go out for fresh air.

Nodding, Warren led Lily to the waterfront where they enjoyed a romantic evening promenade. The sky was studded with millions of stars looking down upon them.

As they sat side-by-side holding each other's hand, Lily marveled at how natural this was. Warren seemed hesitant and a little shy. Deep inside, Lily hoped he didn't mind the hand holding and wished that he were just as eager as she was. Then, when he looked around nervously, Lily understood the reason for his hesitation. While he seemed just as attracted to her as she was to him, Lily surmised Warren was on his guard—he feared they would be caught. Sensing his anxiety, she let go of his hand.

A few minutes later, Lily attempted to make light conversation.

"So you attend Princeton and major in math and physics?" she said.

"Well, they are kind of related in the project I am working on right now," Warren replied.

"Where are you from?" she asked.

"Jackson, Mississippi."

"Your parents live there as well?"

"Just my mother, who's a seamstress. My father is long gone." He looked at her, noticing how the moon cast a glow upon her face. "What about you, Miss Lily?"

"I live in Charleston with my parents. My mother is a piano teacher who teaches students at home," she said, smoothing her skirt. "My father is an engineer presently working around Charleston."

"What do you want to do after you finish high school?"

"Well, I'd like to go to college," she answered coyly, hiding her mouth and nose behind her fan.

Warren's eyes widened. "Your parents will agree to send you to college?"

"Oh, yes, I can go on studying as long as I want."

"That's very gracious of them," Warren said, looking away.

Lily eyed him curiously. "I heard a lot about you from Doug so I won't even bother you with the same question."

He looked straight at her then. "You wouldn't be bothering me at all, Miss Lily."

Lily was especially taken by his olive complexion, tall build, dark wavy hair and dark eyes fringed in long lashes. She couldn't take her eyes off him. She realized that his gaze was equally intent on her.

While it was a bold act for a young lady her age, she moved a little closer to him as they both surveyed the reflection of the fragmented flood lights on the dark water.

All of a sudden, Lily felt his arms wrap around her as she savored the warmth of his touch, the sensuous tingling creeping through her feet, which slowly but surely took over her body. She felt almost limp and gave herself completely to Warren's warm embrace.

They gazed at each other—with his arms still holding her tight as they felt their throbbing hearts pound from chest to chest as the stars twinkled and the moon lay glistening amid the vast sky.

Warren, suddenly startled, freed himself from Lily and nervously uttered, "Miss Lily, I must tell you something."

Disappointed that a single moment could lapse from blissful to stressful, Lily sat still, anxious for what he may reveal.

"If you haven't already observed—I am not entirely white—that is, my mother is white," he said, wiping his sweaty hands on his pants. "My father was black."

He began to move away from her as she sat there stunned. While it came as quite a shock she never expected, still after the initial shock wore off, she brushed it off. "So what?" she said.

It was Warren's turn to look shocked. "It doesn't matter to you?"

Lily tried to assuage his concern with a smile. "Not at all."

Her response still didn't seem to satisfy Warren who began to pace back and forth. "It matters to the world we live in."

She stood up then and placed a reassuring hand on his arm. "We can face the world together."

Warren began to take her hand but thought the better of it. "Miss Lily, I don't want to put you through this."

Lily boldly took both Warren's hands in hers. "You're not doing anything wrong—not to me. We can get through this. I want to be with you."

"Then it's us against the world," he said, sadly as he turned away. "I won't be able to live with myself if the world tortured you just because you chose to be with me."

Lily's fantasy world collapsed like a house of cards. In front of them was the waterfront, still incandescent, still untouched and unhindered by her troubles. Shining like sheet metal, with black lines of ripple, she could see at a distance a steamboat chugged along. The star-crossed couple stood speechless as the gentle summer breeze slowly blew through, unable to lighten their heavy hearts.

"Miss Lily, we should go back to the clubhouse. Doug will be looking for me. He'll notice your absence, too."

Lily found she was unable to stop her tears from rolling down her cheeks.

Whether they would see each other again, Warren took a chance to tell Lily some facts about himself. Then she could decide whether he was worth taking the risk.

"My father was an educated person, earning his living honestly," he said as he cast his eyes toward the water. "He was harassed quite often as a black man. My parents were subject to threats by the neighbors and they had to move from one place to another when I was young. It wasn't a good period in my life."

Warren slowly pulled himself together, held Lily close to him, and uttered softly, "I am really honored by your presence and I will treasure these moments for the rest of my life."

Lily took Warren's two hands and said, "Warren, we could have many more moments like this, if only you'll let us."

They smiled and started walking towards the clubhouse.

"I should tell you more about my family," he said, as they continued walking. "My Grandfather was a slave who worked in the fields and Grandmother worked hard to help him. They were somewhat in good standing with their masters. They raised my father to be educated and ultimately he finished his college education and started teaching math and English in school. His hobby was playing the saxophone in nightclubs."

"My mother was a young and very pretty girl who finished high school but had not yet decided then about her future. She met my father in a concert where he had performed and continued to attend more concerts with her friends not just because she liked the music, but because she had fallen for one of the musicians—my father. It seemed like the perfect love story, nearly a fairy tale, but in reality, it wasn't. They both endured so much and went through life struggling in humiliation all because my father was black and had no money. To add to their misery, my mother's family was closely related to the family where my Grandfather was a slave but later freed. My mother came from a family of old money." Warren paused, his face filled with pain. "Sorry to burden you with this."

Lily was just about to protest when they both crossed paths with Doug, who was walking rather briskly, a worried look on his face. Doug stopped short as soon as he eyed Lily with Warren. A painful, awkward silence ensued as the three young people stood there looking at each other.

Doug seemed to brush off any concern and suspicion he had as he tried to brighten the mood. "Oh there you are! I was looking for you."

"We went out for some fresh air," Lily answered, casting a cautious look toward Warren.

"I see," said Doug as his eyes darted from Lily to Warren and back again. "We have to conclude our party. I'm afraid your curfew looms ahead."

Curfew? Thought Lily. The last time she checked, she was no longer a child. Warren was hesitant to bid farewell to Lily but he knew it was the right thing to do— for now.

"Doug, I'll help you spruce up the place," Warren offered. "Just tell me what needs to be done." Then he turned to Lily, "How are you going to get home? Shall I accompany you?"

Doug hastily said, "That is kind of you to offer, Warren, but there's no need. I'll see to it that she gets home safe and sound."

While Doug was busy with clearing the hall and putting things in place, Warren and Lily secretly exchanged their mailing addresses and promised to keep in touch.

With Doug hovering nearby, it was even a risk to shake hands. So the couple parted with a look of longing just as the stars continued to twinkle as if recording the memory of their evening along with the infinite sky.

When the cousins were alone, Doug, in protective cousin mode, didn't waste any time interrogating Lily, bombarding her with questions.

"Lily, I may have introduced Warren as my friend but I can't say I know very much about his background. I know he is good student and has become one of my good friends these past three years."

"Doug," Lily began, uneasy with her cousin's inquisitive tone. He was obviously fishing for information. She guessed Doug had figured out what went on along the waterfront. "I don't know where you're going with this conversation."

And so, while no more was said that night regarding Warren, Doug made it clear to Lily that while it was fine for him to remain friends with Warren, it would be inappropriate for Lily to stay in contact with the object of her affection.

৩৩৩

As time rolled by, Lily and Warren secretly corresponded through letters until Lily got admitted to Wesleyan College in1927. Meanwhile, Warren had finished his masters and while he was engaged in a research project, he had the intense desire to visit Lily. He just couldn't get her out of his mind, so he wrote to her and she very promptly replied: "I can't wait to see you."

From there began the first of their clandestine meetings. The day of their much-anticipated meeting, the couple exchanged stories about what had occurred since they had last seen each other. To their delight, they found that their feelings for one another had not dissipated. This was for real. So they decided they would continue to meet secretly, away from home, their family and friends and above all, from Doug's suspicious eyes.

During the three days they spent together, they never left each other's side except when Lily had to return to her dorm at the wee hours of the morning to get some sleep.

They arranged visits whenever they had a chance with their busy school schedules and Warren's research. Warren shared the good news to Lily that he was admitted into the doctorate program for physics that would enable him to combine his passion for both physics and math.

While Lily was happy and congratulated him, she wondered what the future held for the both of them. An educated black man still had no right to love a white woman, as society dictated it. Nothing had changed from Warren's parents' generation to theirs. No doubt, there would be struggles ahead.

And that day of reckoning arrived sooner than Lily expected.

Somehow Doug received second-hand information from his close circle of friends about Warren and Lily's secret meetings and their relationship. So as he started inquiring about Warren's mysterious background, Doug realized that he wanted to discover major flaws in Warren's character and reputation that would distance him from Lily. Through intense prodding and investigating, Doug discovered that Warren, who for a long time had fooled everyone into thinking he was of Mediterranean origin, was indeed the son of a black man. That fact definitely put a scar in his book, as far as Doug was concerned.

That particular information made Doug upset and even jealous in a way, that such a man of Warren's background could garner such a high level of achievement, much above his own. Doug knew he could no longer stand by as the world as he knew it was changing before his very eyes. Grabbing his pen, he wrote to Lily.

I am writing to you, as I did not hear from you for a long time. I know you are busy, but it's urgent that I reach you, for there's a matter that needs our utmost attention. You leave me no choice but to break the news to you ever so bluntly. My dear, you should know that Warren is half-black and comes from a poor family. His father is dead. So far, he has managed to pass as white and remain evasive about his social status, choosing to fool us with his somewhat light skin color and excellence in academics. He is hard working and can charm anyone with his good manners. To go further in this relationship with him will be disastrous to you both. As you know, my dear, the social disparity definitely exists and society will never welcome the union. Society will make you an outcast should you chose to continue seeing him. Think about your parents. Do you wish to put them through so much torture? I always loved you like my own baby sister which is why I write, imploring you to distance yourself from Warren at once. I beg

of you. Do this for your family—for your sake. Think about your future.
Best wishes, your loving cousin, Doug

Upon receiving her cousin's letter, Lily became distraught, consumed with anger and sadness. She exploded into a fit of rage and screamed loudly in an empty room, then started sobbing.

"I hate you Doug! You are being unfair and unforgiving. You don't care at all about me. You only care about yourself!"

After her initial explosion, Lily calmed herself down and began thinking deeply, then worriedly as she now feared for Warren's safety. Could he be in trouble? Would Doug even dare to harm Warren himself or enlist other men to do the dirty deed?

The fact that Doug might also attempt to smear Warren's closely guarded reputation occurred to her. Suddenly, Lily remembered what Warren had revealed to her on the night they met—about his parents' struggles as an interracial couple in an intolerable society.

"Oh no! Is his life in danger because of me?" Lily started breathing rapidly with anxiety.

She longed to go to Warren to warn him—to keep him close and safe from harm. Lily sent a telegram to Warren informing him of her plan to rendezvous with her friend, Adriana, acting as chaperone.

The telegram read: "I want to meet you and need to talk urgently. Adriana and I hope to be there by Monday. Love, Lily."

When Lily and Adriana arrived in New Jersey, it had been arranged ahead of time that Lily would stay with Adriana in her parents' home. So before she left, Lily promptly informed Warren the location of where she would stay should she ever be in town on a visit.

With Adriana on hand to cover for Lily's absence, Lily and Warren secretly met at a park not too far from where she stayed. So sad and anxious was she that she burst into tears upon seeing Warren.

They spent few moments of silence hugging each other. To the curious onlooker, Lily knew that Warren could pass as a gentleman from Western Europe, perhaps from France, Spain or Italy, with his olive-skin complexion and Mediterranean good looks. They both settled down and started talking to each other holding hands tightly.

"Lily, we have to finish what we have started," he said, seriously. "This is 1929, you have two more years of college to go and my project will take at least another two years to finish before I can begin writing my dissertation."

She looked up at him with eyes filled with tears. "Whatever are you trying to say? I agree, we will both be busy with our studies but it will be very difficult for me if I lose contact with you and am unable to see you."

Warren shook his head. "Aside from our education, there is the matter of your cousin—your family. This— us—they will never accept. We don't want to look back with regret."

Warren continued holding her hand but Lily sensed that his hold was slipping away.

"Well, we don't want to live a life of regret, either," Lily said. "Did Doug try to contact you?"

Lowering his head, Warren replied, "Yes he did."

"Tell me. What did he write?"

Warren sadly smiled. "Doug is very protective and concerned about you, and also very much concerned about the family regarding the burden they will go through because of us."

Lily put her two elbows on the picnic table and held her head tightly between her palms as she started breathing heavily and sobbing. Her head was throbbing as though it was about to implode.

"Lily, please try to understand, these are the usual reactions one should expect," Warren pleaded. "Our society is not yet ready to accept this kind of relationship. So, we have to do the only thing we have control over— to follow our path to fulfill our dreams. I remember you told me that you wanted to be a writer and I know you will be a famous one, if you tried hard enough. I, too, want to make a mark on the academic world and mathematics is my ticket to acceptance—that which would garner me the respect from my peers that I know I deserve."

Warren went on to express his desire to travel to different academic institutions in the country and lecture on his mathematical theories while trying to provide education to needy students.

As he continued to speak, Lily's heart pounded. She knew he was trying to break it off with her but she wasn't going to allow it.

"We have to see each other, I know it will be challenging, but we will find a way," she said.

She assumed that Warren's silence meant that he agreed with her pleading so, for the time being, she felt consoled. Still, she couldn't help shake off the feeling deep inside her that was telling her that she was asking for the impossible. If they were to succeed at their chosen careers, sacrifices had to be made. She tried to shake off any negative thoughts, preferring instead to relish their few precious, brief moments together.

Lily believed she left New Jersey on a positive note.

⋰⋱⋰⋱⋰⋱

As more time went by, they immersed themselves with their studies, continuing to keep in touch through letters. Nearly a year had passed until they finally reunited briefly during Warren's break from work. He revealed that his mathematical theory was gaining recognition at the university and the obvious joy in Warren's eyes brought joyful tears to her own. More time had passed until they decided to meet again, this time around Wesleyan where Lily was finishing her studies.

By this time, Lily was overwhelmed with emotion as she hugged and kissed Warren, not letting her eyes off him for a minute. She truly felt that, since they had come this far in their relationship, anything was possible.

After an initial period of joy and excitement, they discussed their further academic plans that included Warren finishing his dissertation and Lily starting to fulfill her dream of writing for the campus newspaper. Since it seemed that the "sky's the limit," she was determined to get a master's degree, perhaps at Warren's university so she could be close to him.

But alas, their joy was brief. Warren seemed to be anxious and sad. He started to say something but stopped, so an equally anxious Lily inquired, "Tell me, what is going on with you? You know, you can tell me anything."

Warren remained silent and distant. At Lily's insistence, he finally spilled out the words he dreaded sharing with her.

"I got an anonymous letter from someone stating that I will be in danger if I don't watch out. The writer stated that a colored man had no business masquerading as a white man and further threatened to expose me, an act that would surely bring serious consequences."

Lily voice cracked with fear as she asked, "When did you receive this letter?"

"About few weeks ago," Warren replied. "But I didn't want to worry you. Now, I think you need to know as I fear for your safety as well as my own."

"Do you think Doug sent it?" she asked, knowing full well that if he did she will never forgive her cousin. "What do you think we should do?"

"The postmark is from New York," Warren replied, solemnly. "It could be anyone but surely it's from someone privy to our secret visits. It's difficult to trust anyone these days."

Finally, Lily realized the gravity of their situation—what Warren had predicted all along. As much as she tried to remain optimistic about their future, at the moment, a future together—as husband and wife seemed bleak at best. The thought that their lives would forever be in danger began to take its toll on Lily who appeared to be shaken from her very core.

"I don't want to lose you. I can't bear to be without you."

Warren, on the other hand, seemed to be calm outside, perhaps for Lily's sake, but inside he was seething.

"This means more than not being able to attend your graduation," Warren said. "Can't you finally see that society won't allow us to be together? Not now and perhaps, not ever."

"Forget about my graduation, I am very much concerned about your well being," she said, still in denial that they were not destined to be together no matter what the circumstances.

Lily had to admit—she was quite headstrong for his taste. No matter what Warren would say to reason with her, she had strived to figure out a way for them to continue to meet and communicate. Once again, she convinced Warren that they could manage to keep their relationship a secret, despite the threats, as long as they could be very careful.

❦❦❦

Lily's final year of college proved to be hectic and in the meantime, Warren was busy wrapping up his research and dissertation. Yet, they still managed to keep in touch through discreetly and cautiously sent letters that had fake names inscribed in the letters as well as the envelopes should the letters fall into the wrong hands.

Soon, Lily graduated with flying colors and was in a high spirits, looking forward to graduate study. She returned home for a much-deserved break in the summer of 1931.

Doug had been keeping busy setting up his own business of selling building material. But he was never too busy to keep a watchful eye on Lily.

Open discussion with her parents about her future and getting a life partner opened a Pandora's Box. Her mother became upset and hysterical as she sobbed and blamed her husband for granting too much freedom to their daughter. Lily's mother said she already knew about "the colored man" whom Doug had mentioned. Lily looked toward her father, searching for some sign of support, but he could not provide any, as he remained silent under his stoic demeanor. Lily seemed to accept her parents' expected behavior toward their daughter's revelation and they even told her that, within time, she would get over this ridiculous phase of her life and eventually move on. Lily believed that now, her only escape was to gain admission to graduate school. *Why I hadn't thought about this before*, she thought.

Lily went to bed that summer night eager to wake up refreshed and eager to seize her pen to write to Warren about a brilliant plan for them to elope without further delay. But when Lily's mother had suffered a mild stroke, leaving one side of her body paralyzed, Lily felt guilty and remained with her mother until she regained her strength.

All the while, Lily remained concerned about Warren. She found out that was constantly being harassed by people outside the university campus who apparently heard word about his "hidden identity" as a colored man. Thankfully, there were a few people who were sympathetic to Warren's plight, including his research mentor, who took pity on Warren and gave him a place to room and board until he was ready to leave for a teaching job elsewhere.

৯৯৯

It seemed that destiny would not rule in their favor. After some time, correspondence between Lily and Warren began to wane, and through the grapevine, Lily knew that Warren had accepted a teaching position at Howard University just as Lily was accepted to graduate school in Chapel Hill, North Carolina.

Lily's departure from home caused a surge of bittersweet and ambivalent feelings. She blamed herself for her mother's disability after her relationship with Warren was revealed. But on the other hand, she scorned the hypocrisy of society and her family for not truly caring their daughter's well being, preserving only their pride and prejudices. Such utter nonsense, she thought.

So much for proclaiming that all men are created equal. As far as I'm concerned, it's all damn rubbish, she thought.

Her graduate school years at Chapel Hill kept her mind occupied and Lily embraced the challenge as it helped her cope with her personal anguish over her forbidden love.

To stay sane, Lily focused on her family obligations and her studies. She finished graduate school with flying colors; ready to launch a lucrative career in writing.

Except for getting a job as a reporter for the local newspaper, several years rolled by without incident, as Lily remained focused on her career, trying to put the past behind her as her fond memories of Warren caused much sadness.

One time, Lily heard that Warren would be lecturing at UNC-Chapel Hill. She made a point to attend the lecture secretly. This was one opportunity she could not ignore. She felt that after much time had gone by, society had forgiven its social ills of yesterday—but she had not forgotten.

As the lights dimmed in the lecture hall, when she was safely ensconced in her seat blending in with the audience, Lily gasped as Warren stepped on stage. He was still as handsome as she remembered him. From her vantage point, she was close enough to see that a few strands of grey accented by the spotlight had weaved through his thick, wavy black hair, but she was too far from him to gauge how happy he was—if indeed he was happy, that is.

Their brief stolen moments together were forever etched in her memory. Inside their aging bodies, their hearts still remained forever young. At one point during the lecture, Warren paused as his eyes scanned the audience. Lily's heart throbbed so violently in her chest she swore the man seated next to her could hear it. Then, as if drawn by some unseen magnetic force, their eyes met and locked. It was then that their love was sealed with just one weighted look that carried several unspoken words of love.

As soon as the lecture was over, Warren, surrounded by a swarm of students, faculty, admirers of his work, stood amid the crowd watching Lily walking up the aisle toward the exit. As she glanced back, they exchanged one last look before the crowd, eager to get Warren's attention, swallowed him and it was impossible to see him. She exited the lecture hall, satisfied to get one more glimpse of him, but still sad nonetheless.

Lily used her journalistic connections to find out what Warren had been up to. She'd heard and read that he became a famous mathematician who still taught at Howard University and was frequently invited to different universities in the U.S and abroad to lecture on the mathematical theory he founded. To her utter disappointment, Lily found that Warren had been happily married to a black woman from Georgia, an elementary school teacher who bore him four beautiful children. It was undisputable proof that he had indeed moved on while she had not.

As for Lily—she never found a suitable match. It seemed that after Warren, no other man would do. Despite her success as a reporter and all the books she published and the places she traveled, the one thing that eluded her kept her cup only half full.

Upon their passing, her parents, perhaps laden with guilt over their daughter's inability to find love again, left her a very generous gift—her family home. It became her safe haven, a place where she could write uninterrupted, and finally be her very best self. The house became Lily's constant source of joy, her pet project, a place that kept her occupied well into her later years as she enjoyed her success as one of America's most notable women authors—quite a feat for a Southern woman who was once confined to society's expectations of her pedigree.

The house, and her Golden Retriever, Macy, became her trusted companions as she continued to pour her heart on paper. Would she ever write about her ill-fated romance? Only time would tell. But for now, she knew that no matter what life held, her treasured memories would always remain where they truly belonged—in her heart.

One day, destiny arrived in the form of a letter, a solitary response to her heart's desire. Deep inside her middle-aged body, her youthful heart pounded as she opened the envelope. Warren wrote that his wife had passed some years ago and that since their brief encounter at Chapel Hill—since they first met—he realized he had never stopped thinking about her.

> My Dearest Lily:
> You were right all along; I should've listened to you. I shouldn't have shrunk back in fear of what society dictated and while we both went our separate ways, I want you to know, I've always carried you in my heart.
> I'm going to be in your town to give a lecture. I wish to see you; that is, if you will still have me.
> Eternally yours, Warren

Her heart started to beat faster as her hands and feet tingled. As she saw two birds perched side by side on a branch of a tree chirping happily, she saw beyond her past to what lay ahead and smiled.

Grandpa's
Sunday Shakespeare Scholars

On a lazy Sunday, despite a screen of fog, the day remained cold and crisp as the sun started smiling on the earth. Amrita sat outside on her backyard deck enjoying nature with her sight and senses.

Mother Nature had teased and taunted the dry earth for some time. It was winter in northern California and there were clouds in the sky, but no rain had fallen. Nevertheless, a feeling of deep calm overshadowed the restlessness of the land and people.

A gentle breeze stirred the wind chimes hanging among the last few leaves on a persimmon tree. She watched as a group of doves landed on her deck, some of them fluttering about, giving her a strange look.

"Oh," she realized, "I forgot to put out some seeds for them." This sparked a vivid memory. Soon she was enveloped by a vision of the time when she was in the eighth grade. Every Sunday she would feed the pigeons in the backyard of her childhood home in Calcutta. And, every other Sunday morning, Amrita would visit her maternal Grandparents' home where her Grandpa would offer tutorials to college students majoring in English.

Knowing Amrita's great interest in English literature, her Grandpa told her mother that she could attend the tutorial. This would also give Amrita a chance to visit frequently with her Grandparents, to whom she was extremely close.

While for practical reasons, Amrita was encouraged by her parents to pursue studies and a career in science (which she would eventually do) her first love was classic literature. Her Grandparents knew this and the reason behind it. Amrita's mother, who was a writer and editor of a journal, invited local writers and poets to get together four times a year at their house. At each gathering, there would be a competition among the students on how many classics they had read and how much poetry they could recite. This always inspired Amrita.

While the tutorial was scheduled to start at ten in the morning and was supposed to last two hours, it usually took longer as Grandpa's students were very enthusiastic, had numerous questions and were adamant about asserting their points-of-view.

After breakfast Amrita was ready to go while her mother would say, "Drink your glass of milk and take the money I laid out for you. And, you're not walking over there this time, young lady."

"Walking is good and I enjoy walking," Amrita objected.

"I know, but it makes you tired and there are projects you have to do for school," her mother replied.

Her mother was unaware that the main reason Amrita didn't take the bus was to save money for a little boy whose father was a roadside peddler. The boy would sit by his father and concentrate on his studies, while his father sold various items to the passersby. A tattered, borrowed book was his constant companion.

On her way back from her Grandparents, Amrita would often visit with this young scholar. One evening, Amrita saw him studying by the roadside under the streetlights, surrounded by a cacophony of noises from passing buses and cars. The ebb and flow of chattering pedestrians could not distract him.

"Why do you study here?" Amrita asked.

"My mother works, too, so I do not want to be home alone," the boy replied.

"How are you doing otherwise?"

"Fine," the boy replied. "I'm learning this poetry by heart because I'm going to recite it in school."

"That's nice to hear," said Amrita, proud of this self-motivated student. Amrita would hand over her two weeks' saving of her bus fare to his father and say, "Please accept my little gift and buy something—whatever you feel is necessary for him."

"Thank you, I will buy the book he needs," said the boy's father. The little boy's bright black eyes shone like twin candles on a dark night.

Amrita had to hurry, so she started running, skipping and when she got tired, she'd walk fast until she arrived at Grandpa's house, situated in a cozy, quiet corner of the south part of Calcutta. Amrita always felt at home in this cottage with its sheltering trees and flowering plants. The backyard boasted of Grandpa's garden on one side with fragrant roses identified by nametags. The other corner of the garden featured Grandma's vegetables and herbs.

The room where the tutorials were held had wide doors and windows, which were opened to the backyard. Most of the time there were fragrant white tuberoses in a long slender vase. There was a carpet with an intricate design and padded mats on the floor to sit on, which lent an air of coziness to the room. Each student had a polished wooden desk that featured grooves on the desktop to hold a pen and pencil. Students would sit in lotus position with the desks within reach for easy access.

There was a blackboard on one wall of the room, but the main attraction were the tall bookcases packed with books. Housed within their shelves was a series of leather-bound Shakespeare dramas: Macbeth, Othello, Merchant of Venice—all published by Yale University Press. The selection of poetry books bound in chocolate-colored leather featured titles engraved in gold-plated lettering, including the works of Wordsworth, Shelley, Keats, Browning, Tennyson and a host of other notable poets. Classic bound books of Bankim Chandra and Sarat Chandra, famous Indian writers, joined the selections of poem and short stories by Rabindranath Tagore. Pictures of Shakespeare, Shelley and Tagore adorned the walls.

As the students settled into their seats, Amrita went straight inside to give her Grandparents a big hug, then she was ready for class. The sessions were always intriguing and intellectually stimulating. Some days there would be poetry selections, showcasing Amrita's favorites including Tennyson, Wordsworth, Shelley and Keats. Best of all, she loved to listen to her Grandpa's recitation of the various poems.

Grandpa, who was five-feet-ten inches tall with olive colored skin, a sharp nose and very bright black eyes, would always wear a black prince coat and gray pants. When he entered, his presence would brighten the room. Grandpa came from a family of educators. Amrita's Great-Grandfather was a Sanskrit scholar who taught the graduate program at the University of Calcutta. Grandpa's elder brother was head of the department of English in a college in south Calcutta, while for many years Grandpa had been an English teacher at the Scottish church college located in north Calcutta.

Amrita sat in front and the students would spoil her with affection and praise. Grandpa would recite Tennyson and the "Rhyme of the Ancient Mariner" by Coleridge. She loved hearing the word "albatross." Amrita would imagine a big bird and a ship cruising along the deep blue sea. Amrita and all the students were fascinated by Shakespeare's dramas and each semester they would choose a particular play to perform. One of the students raised his hand.

"Yes, Kiran, you have a question?" Grandpa asked.

"Sir, I just want to know the mechanics and technical challenge of Shakespeare Walla."

"Well, Mrinal and Bimal are very much well-versed with it so they can explain it to you," Grandpa suggested.

Among the students there were few who went to professional acting classes and were members of a company called "Shakespeare Walla," which meant those who sold Shakespeare's drama. In this group, members would go to small towns in remote parts of the country and stage a particular Shakespeare play.

"We are staging 'The Merchant of Venice' in Bongaon," Barun, one of the student actors said. Bongaon, Amrita knew, was a town about one hundred kilometers from Kolkata located at the border of East Pakistan, presently known as Bangladesh. "You are welcome to come and join us. The drama group has invited us there, and the mayor of the town has shown much interest."

"Thank you," said Amrita. "I'd be very interested, but I will need to ask the permission of my parents."

"Of course," replied Barun. He continued his questions. "Sir, when was 'The Merchant of Venice' written?"

"To my knowledge, it was written between 1594 and 1598," Grandpa responded.

Fascinated by her Grandpa's answers to all of the students' questions, Amrita would write down all the answers.

"During that time," Grandpa continued, "Well-known writer Francis Meyers published his *Palladis Tamia* where, in contrast to classic English poets, he mentions Shakespeare as a leading contemporary dramatist."

"Sir, is there a source for this play or is it the completely new invention of William Shakespeare?" asked Subrata, one of the actors in 'The Merchant of Venice.'

"The chief source is probably an Italian work, *Il Pecorone,* written in 1378 by Giovanni Florentino and published in 1565," Grandpa answered. "England was familiar with large numbers of vernacular translations from the Italian; it is probable that Shakespeare had access to one in this instance."

After two-and-a-half hours of intellectual discourse Grandpa would look at her and announce, "Didimoni, it is time for a break!" ('Didimoni' was Grandpa's special nickname for Amitra.) This was the indication that delicious food would soon be offered. Menus would be different every Sunday and Amrita would wait eagerly until Grandpa recited what Grandma had made. A typical Sunday would feature *chapati*, or *parantha*, with vegetable curry with cauliflower peas and potato. Fried fish dipped in batter or prawn cutlet would also be offered. Fruit would be sliced, chilled with mango, and dessert featured rice pudding, or *Rasha Malay.*

Amrita enjoyed chatting with her grandparents as she devoured the delicious food. The conversation would center on school, friends or whatever accomplishments she had that week. Grandma and Grandpa were very pleased when Amrita mentioned that she wanted to take some warm food they had for their lunch for the little boy who studied alongside his father.

Grandpa eyes sparkled with joy. "Didimoni, it is very gracious of you to give what you can."

"Please do it humbly, you are not giving only but receiving also," said Amrita's Grandma, who was five-feet-three inches tall and who used to put a red vermillion *bindi* in the middle of her forehead. Her round face glowed like the morning sun. She adorned her bright-bordered white saris with gold jewelry that enhanced her beauty. Her long black hair was tucked in a bun complementing her traditional attire.

One particular day after a tutorial, Amrita requested Grandpa to share a story about the time he was put into prison by the British Regime because they assumed that he was the leader of a revolutionary student movement. The student movement that was going on at that time was against British Raj, before India's Independence took place from 1944 to 1947. The students rebelled against the British and attacked a district judge at the outskirts of Calcutta where Grandpa used to teach English at the district school.

"The night was dark and very quiet," Grandpa began, "as the children were away with their Grand-parents. Suddenly there was sound of marching boots and a terrible noise as if someone was digging at the yard. There were searchlights moving around the house giving an eerie feeling of dread. I saw that the house was surrounded by armed men in uniform. One man came and kicked the door. Others started banging on the windows. They were shouting, 'Open the door and come out with hands up!' "

He recounted that he and Grandma came out slowly with their hands up.

"Then they put shackles on my feet and around my waist and arrested me," he said. "Then they announced that I had weapons hidden underground and showed some rifles which never belonged to me."

Grandpa explained that while he stood in shock at the accusation, his wife shouted, "Those do not belong to us!"

But the men shouted back: "Shut up or we are going to put shackles on you, too." The men then entered the house and dismantled everything without a search warrant.

"It was eerily quiet after those men dragged Grandpa to their van," said Grandma who added her memory of the incident. "I thought I was having a bad dream. But it was a nightmare."

Eventually, Grandpa was released.

"I did not give up," Grandpa said. "Initially, I borrowed some money as the British government froze all the money in our bank. Gradually, I started earning money by teaching students privately."

"Did those people come back to harass you?" Amrita asked.

"Yes, they did. They asked all kinds of questions and the secret service would follow me in the evening, even if I was just getting groceries."

Amrita was overwhelmed with emotion.

"Freedom does not come free," said Grandpa.

"Our generation went through much hardship and fought for your freedom and the freedom of future generations," Grandma added.

The lulling murmur from the branches of trees outside the window was suddenly interrupted by the coarse and dissonant sound of a motorbike roaring through the neighborhood. The echo of the past suddenly dissipated and Amrita felt as though she just awakened from a dream. Reluctantly, Amrita came back to the present.

A gentle breeze blew through the barren leaves, as the sun started moving towards the west. The wind chimes slowly started up its tune. The little birds hopped around and a squirrel jumped from one branch to another. The clouds sailed through the mist on their way to Mount Diablo, the majestic mountain that Amrita had the pleasure of viewing from the deck of her backyard.

For a moment, amid the fluffy clouds cruising along the horizon, she thought could see the faces of her Grandparents on the clouds smiling down at her.

Ode to Mysterium

The summer evening settled in just as the maple trees started to move their limbs and the birch tree with its long slender trunk, gently swayed. The blue jays were chirping a long conversation on one of the branches.

Two squirrels suddenly stopped jumping; it seemed they were about to retire for the day. Slowly the shadow of darkness fell over the hills and meadows. The soft touch of the cool breeze reminded me of some past story of a unique place.

The story was about a lake up in the Himalayas, located at the northern part, almost at the border of India and China. A long time ago, I saw a slide show about this lake called Manas Sarovar. The water of this lake is dark blue like an ocean. In this lake the big blue lotuses grow, and nowhere else in the world could you ever find such beautiful things.

The sweet fragrance of the lotuses would carry you to a different perspective where you would forget all your worries and anxieties of daily life. These thoughts and imaginations were slowly creeping all over me. The big red moon appeared up beyond Mount Diablo. The stars appeared one by one on the horizon and the devilish mountain, Diablo, moved further and further away from my sight until it stood at a distance like a ghostly shadow.

My eyes were getting tired. I saw misty shadows of the trees, that looked like figures wrapped in white chiffon, swaying with their outstretched branches, whispering, *I wonder what is happening? Am I dreaming? The mountain seems to be moving backwards away from my sight.*

I heard a faint voice, calling my name from a distance.

"Who is that calling me?"

"I am your friend—do not be afraid," said the voice.

"Why are you here and why are you calling me?"

"I did not call you. I came as you wanted me to come," replied a lady who suddenly appeared in front of me.

"This is very strange—I do not know you and never saw you so how could I ask you to come?"

The lady wore a long orange dress, her long brown hair almost touching her knees. She was about five-feet-five inches tall with olive colored skin, and a sharp-pointed nose. Her big hazel eyes sparkled.

She seemed a bit familiar to me, yet I could not imagine why. Did she look like a familiar painting I saw somewhere? It bothered me for a few moments and then I started talking again.

"My name is Pushpita. What is your name?" I asked.

"My friend, you do not need to be bothered with any name. You do not need to call me anything. I ask that you follow me for I will take you to places you have never been and would never reach without me," the unknown lady replied.

With a suspicious look, I asked her, "Why are you volunteering to take me and why should I go when I do not even know who you are?"

"My dear, you wanted to go somewhere for a long time and see faraway lands with your own eyes, remember?" the lady replied.

"What are you talking about?" I asked her.

"Oh my dear Pushpita, you will find out," the lady answered with a smile.

Some unseen energy was pushing me forward. I could see that I had no other alternative than to follow her. It very early in the morning. There was light on the eastern horizon and I guessed the sun would be up soon. The path we took was winding up the mountain; on either side there were big pine trees and shrubs. Down below, a river was flowing busily through the rocks and boulders. A flock of birds flew over and broke the silence.   At a distance I saw the flowering rhododendrons color the landscape in red. We passed a murmuring brook, which slid through the rocks. We both climbed quite a steep terrain. Around us, there were ranges of mountain peaks covered with snow. One could hear a vibration of unknown origin, which echoed through the mountains. I was moved with the peace and tranquility. Time stopped, as I was completely absorbed in that moment.

"These are the ranges of the Himalayas," said the lady.

"The Himalayas? That's far." I was just thinking how I arrived here.

I kept on moving. There were so many flowering plants on either side; some looked like small sunflowers—others looked like bluebells. Daisies of different colors and sizes were in abundance.

"Pushpita, do you see the famous big lake, the one you always wanted to see?"

"What do you mean?" I asked.

"I mean, this is Manas Sarovar," the lady replied.

I was really confused and excited at the same time. I just wanted to reach there and see it with my own eyes. We came very close to the bank, which was quite enormous, as far as the eye could see. It was sapphire blue and the reflected red of the eastern sky broke in pieces and started sparkling on the ripples of the blue water. Oh yes, there were the blue lotuses floating here and there around the edges, along with their big green leaves. The sweet fragrance I heard about was said to take you to some other dimension where you would forget all your worries. I was completely absorbed with the unique sight.

"Wait, there are more surprises," the lady said.

My feet and fingers were cold, with an unknown anxiety. "What's coming next?"

"You know Alexander Scriabin is here and presenting his musical debut," she said.

I wondered why she mentioned the famous Russian composer who had been long dead. "Sasha, as

Scriabin was fondly known, lived from 1871 to 1915. He wanted to perform his music in India."

The lady nodded. "Yes, it is true that he wanted to perform especially here."

My blood started to boil. What was this woman hinting at? "Are you joking? Do you think I'm a fool?"

The woman sighed. "Do not get upset. Just relax. I know you are very interested in Sasha's music and also fascinated to know his life and have questions about his intention to perform in India, where you were born."

I was curious about the lady's connection to Scriabin. "Did you know him personally? Were you related to him? You address him by his pet name as if you were close to him." I gave an inquisitive look.

As the cool breeze blew through the lady's long brown hair, she arranged her strands away from her forehead and replied with a smile, "Ah, but my dear, you will find out soon enough. Tell me, Pushpita, what do you think of my Sasha?"

Hmmm. I was becoming highly suspicious of her tone. What did she mean by *her* Sasha? I wondered why she kept repeating Scriabin's pet name and fondly addressing him as "Sasha" as if she was his mother.

The idea that this figure could be Scriabin's mother came to my mind and struck me like lightning. I felt nervous and bewildered, then I tried to compose myself.

When I was ready to speak to her, I looked her straight in the eye and said, "My opinion of Maestro Scriabin stems from the impression of the people around him at that time and later when people commented about him and his music compositions." I sighed. It was a challenge to briefly answer the lady's question.

"Here's my take on Alexander Scriabin: he was a controversial Russian composer, one of the visionary pioneers who sought a new musical language, a full decade before the advances of Stravinsky and Schoenberg," I said, looking far into the horizon past the lady who eyed me curiously.

She stood quietly observing me as I shared more of my impressions of the Russian composer who searched for a way to express, through sound, the mystical and theosophical ideals that obsessed him. To me, Scriabin was a pianist, composer, theosophist, philosopher, poet and mystic. The mystic aspect of him especially fascinated me as I am from India, land of the enchanted mystics.

"That is wonderful that you and your generation has given so much thought about my Sasha's music," said the lady. "I get the impression that you love his music. He did not expect that he would have such a huge following of the kind of music he was composing. He just composed for the sake of composing, his love of music constantly ringing melodiously all the time inside his head." The woman cast a faraway look.

Thoughts came rushing to my mind. Beyond the facts, how does she seem to know "Sasha" so intimately? *Did you spend a lot of time with him?*

The question, which I silently asked myself, must have escaped from my lips as she looked at me and smiled sadly.

"No. Not really," she said. "He was very lucky to have an aunt accompany him all the time whenever he needed. But it is true, my dear, I watched him from afar when he would get restless with the ringing of musical notes in his head and I somehow inspired him to continue his composition. The music would pour forth and take shape in various forms." The lady looked at me and she smiled.

I was not comfortable with all the mysterious energy surrounding me. It felt eerie.

Suddenly there was the sound of the performance.

The Symphony – The Divine Poem.

The performance went on with the sound of the Poem of Ecstasy.

But the Poem of Fire started with lights reflected like fire. My body was numb; it was a feeling of fear, sadness and joy at the same time like the colors of flame. It was not real and I knew it in my heart, but did not want it to end.

At this point, since the lady's arrival and her admission over her mysterious connection with the great composer, I found myself asking: "Please, dear lady, you appear to have known him and know him still, perhaps in a past life and in this life. If it is possible," my heart pounded, "Can I meet him?"

The lady pursed her lips as if she kept a valuable secret.

"Yes, you can not only meet him but you may talk to him as well," the lady replied.

I had to pinch myself to make sure I wasn't imagining all of this. A while ago I had taken a piano literature class on Scriabin. I found it to be powerful as I started hearing those pieces, some of which were short; and like the autumn leaves that landed in front of me, you just enjoyed the beauty and the colors at the same time.

I was overwhelmed with emotion, as my heart started beating faster with joy and anticipation at the same time.

Yes, I could see the Maestro from a distance. Cleft chin, upturned nose, soft eyes set in a broad and bearded Slavic face wreathed in bronze-glinted brown hair.

"I see the man himself," I breathed. "The composer, pianist, poet, mystic, theosophist and philosopher—the one and only and in the flesh, no less."

I didn't think the man that I was slowly approaching was actually an actual flesh and blood creature. Nonetheless, I followed my mysterious female companion near the figure, which looked like Scriabin to me.

Looking at me through hooded eyes, he stood there, regarding me as if I was a strange specimen. "I know you wanted to know about me and my dear mother," Scriabin said.

I'm quite sure he caught my surprised expression and silly smile.

The composer held out his hand, gesturing us to take our seats on plush chairs and tables that seem to appear out of nowhere.

Scriabin tilted his head, resting his right cheek on his right fist as his right elbow rested on a shiny surface of an oval tabletop.

"My *papasha*, my father, Nikolai Alexandrovich, after two years of Moscow University life, used to spend summer in the country," Scriabin said.

He went on to say that in 1870, he was in Bernov midway along the railway line connecting Moscow and Petersburg.

"There was another attraction there for him—a girl named Lyubov Petrovna—who played the piano seriously," Scriabin said. "Papasha fell in love."

He continued his family narrative saying it was quite remarkable in his mother Lyubov's day and for women in her generation to achieve the great honor of being one of the first lady musicians of Russia. She graduated in 1867 from the Petersburg conservatory with honors, garnering the Great Gold Medal and the diploma of the Free Artist. She knew Anton Rubinstein as "Little Papa" and he reciprocated with an intimate "Little Daughter" moniker. Her piano teacher was no less than Theodor Leschetizky, the most lauded pedagogue of Europe.

"Yes, Maestro, I heard she was a great musician and pianist in her own right," I said with all sincerity.

He stopped and carefully regarded my lady companion.

"I wonder if you could please tell me about a concert where she played a full program while she was seven months pregnant and the proceeds were donated toward the building of the first shelter house for the juvenile delinquents," I said, my fingers interlaced.

Maestro Scriabin burst into huge laughter.

I was very uncomfortable; I thought I had done something wrong.

"Do not be impatient my child. I haven't gotten to the part of the story where she gets married to my father first." He scratched his beard, a thoughtful, faraway look in his eyes.

Continuing his story in the autumn of 1870, the composer relayed that Nikolai and Lyubov got married and by October 1871, Lyubov was seven months pregnant when she performed a full program of Scarlatti's Sonata, Chopin's Ballad and Etude, pieces by Leschetizky, Schumann, Wagner, Liszt, and at the end played a scherzo composed by her. Tirelessly, Lyubov played another solo concert five days before her baby was born.

"I thought it was quite reckless for Lyubov to perform the difficult pieces in front of the public wearing constricting evening attire with a baby on the way," Scriabin said. "My *papasha* and my mama had to reach

Moscow in time for the traditional patriarchal style of the parents' confinement at the house."

He stated further that the railway ride was jarring with sporadic stops at all hours of the day and night. The cold grew extreme as they traveled further north.

"My mother caught a cold and a hacking cough," the composer said, his voice becoming glum. "Ultimately they reached Moscow on December 25th. She was so ill that she had to be carried upstairs to the bedroom. "I heard this sad story from my aunt, my father's sister, named Lyubov Alexandrova who looked after me all her life and never got married."

Scriabin said that his aunt told him that Christmas day, 1871 in Moscow was a gaudy, noisy celebration. Church and partygoers crowded the streets all day, dropping in on friends to eat little cakes and rolled pancakes. The churches rang cannonades of bells for each three solemn Christmas day masses.

Golden cupolas in sunlight glittered the skyline with flashing luminous bulbs. Snow crusts on rooftops and windowsills crackled and snapped as the sun shone steadily. The freezing cold was dry, crisp and stimulating.

Inside the Scriabin house the anxiety of clouds hushed the exuberance. There was no music that Christmas, only silent waiting.

"Then at two in the afternoon on December 25, 1871, I was born."

On New Year's Eve the baby boy was christened Alexander Nikolayevich Scriabin. The health of his mother grew worse day by day and ten days after birth the doctor discovered that her lungs were badly inflamed. To prevent the contagion, Grandmother Elisabeth transferred the baby and his nurse to her room.

"In Aunt Lyubov's diary she stated 'that little Shurinka' became our property," he said, shaking his head sadly. It was said that my mother improved for a short period of time. The doctors finally despaired. He recommended that my father take my mother, as a last desperate hope, to Europe where 'the climate is merciful.' So my father took her to Arco, a tiny town in the Dolomites which lies at the one edge of the beautiful lake Garda."

The composer's breathing became so heavy that he had to hold the arm of the chair for support before continuing his story.

"Unfortunately, nothing worked and Lyubov Petrovna, my dearest mother, died at the age of twenty-three and she was buried there," Scriabin said.

He admitted that he extracted more facts from his aunt Lyubov's diary. "She wrote urging my father to return to Moscow alone and that her devotion to Shurinka grew," Scriabin said. "My Aunt Lyubov said that her love for her young nephew was so strong that she even forgot that she was still young enough to bear a child of her own."

The composer picked up a book from the table. It was his Aunt Lyubov's diary. He opened the diary and cleared his throat then read: "Whenever a proposal of marriage was expressed, I had only to take a look at that infant to realize I would be separated from him. I could not face such loneliness, however rosy the future might seem."

As Maestro Scriabin closed the book, he sighed. "All that is left of my mother was an oil painting of her done by her brother—my uncle. I never parted with that painting of her. I keep that close to me."

Scriabin took a deep breath and looked at a distance. "Anything else you want to know, my child?"

It was my turn to sigh. It was tragic to lose his young, talented mother. "Yes, Maestro—why did you decide to come to India and perform your musical debut?"

Scriabin looked lost in thought. "I'm happy to tell you why but it may be very difficult for you to enter the realm of my understanding."

"I might not understand exactly and fully, but I will still grasp the essence of it as India is my birthplace," I said, hoping to convince him.

"You see my mind travels millions of miles, in split seconds. So when I explain things it might not feel like I am explaining something," he said. "That person has to fill in the blanks, as I try to run fast. But for you, I will try to make it simpler."

I sat on the edge of my seat, prepared to hear him rhapsodize about my country.

"India to me is land of sages, sadhus, magical, mystifying attainments and not the trickery of rope tricks and snake charmers only. The perfume of a tropical flower is all I need to smell to forget my present. The savory tropical fruit to make me remember what I am hungry for. At the foot of the Himalayas, snow moderates the heat and sunset and dawns can be incorporated into prefatory action."

The composer paused momentarily and shot me a curious look.

"You know my work, *Mysterium*?"

I eagerly nodded. "Yes, I heard about it, Maestro. You wanted to explore the sense of touch smell and hearing."

The Maestro's eyes lit up passionately. "Listen to me my child, there will not be a single spectator. All will be participants. The work requires special artists—a completely new culture. The cast of performers includes an orchestra, a large mixed choir, instruments with visual effects, dancers, a procession, incense, and rhythmic textural, articulation. The cathedral in which it will take place will not be of one single type of stone but will continually change with the atmosphere and motion of *Mysterium*. This will be done with the aid of mist and light. Bells suspended from clouds, will start to ring, sunrise will be the preludes and sunsets will be codas."

He paused again and looked at me.

"This may all sound so esoteric, but did you get anything from my statement?"

I nodded. "Maestro, I might not totally understand the myriad nuances of your genius, but I come from a land of mysticism, a realm where special mantras and rituals by people bring rain, musical ragas can create fire and travel a long distance to bring back lost loved ones."

"Ah, there you see," the Maestro said. "When you listen closely, you'll find not a musical drama or presentation, but a direct experience where soul and matter will separate under high tension induced by music's vibration. Human beings would be transfigured into an endless, deepest ocean. Through this musical experience, all of us would be immersed in another time, transported to an ecstatic abyss of sunshine."

Beyond his compositions, I found the Maestro's words to be sheer music to my ears and shared with him what I knew about his world.

"Maestro, for a long time musicians and scientists were trying to find the connection between the music and color," I relayed. "The 17th–century physicist Isaac Newton tried to solve the problem by assuming that musical and color tones have frequencies in common. According to Newton, the distribution of white light in a spectrum of colors is analogous to musical distribution of tones in an octave. So, he identified seven discrete light entities, he then matched them to the seven discrete notes of an octave. What do think about this theory?"

Maestro looked at me in what I hoped was a sign he was impressed with my knowledge. "Yes, I detect your enthusiasm by your theory you presented. But I can see and perceive the senses myself and I can see the color in musical note, and this is my theory that when the correct color is perceived with correct sound, it becomes a powerful resonator to the listener." He scratched his bearded chin as he narrowed his eyes. "Have you heard *Prometheus, Poem of Fire?*"

"I have heard of it, Maestro."

"You must understand that music and visual imagery come very naturally to me," he said. "That is why I want to perform in India. Bells suspended from the clouds in the sky would summon the spectators from all over the world. The performance would take place in a half temple built in India."

Scriabin further expressed his desire that a reflecting pool of water would complete the divinity of the half-circle stage. The seating will be strictly graded ranking radially from center to the stage, where the composer would sit at the piano, surrounded by hosts of instruments, singers and dancers. The choreography would include glances, looks and eye movements and touches of hand movements, odors of pleasant perfumes, frankincense, and constantly changing lighting effects would pervade the cast and the audience.

"I am preparing myself with yogic exercises," Scriabin happily noted. "India would revive my soul, awaken my feelings and heighten my receptivity. I would see the world in a different perspective. The contemporary India does not attract me, but I know I could push through all these odds to those real feelings and experiences which the real India expresses and embodies in space."

The composer paused, eyeing me carefully. "I fear all that I'm presenting to you may be quite overwhelming."

I shook my head. "Please, Maestro, I'm hanging on to every word. Do not fear that you will lose my interest."

"I have to admit, it's a lot to take in but I think it should slowly permeate, like the scent of jasmine," he said. Then he turned his attention to the woman who served as my guide.

"I see this lovely woman has guided you to me," Scriabin said. "Given all that I've told you thus far, and your willingness to be open to all magical possibilities of this realm, would you be so shocked to hear that, after all this time, your lady guide who sought you out, knowing your interest in me and brought you here, is no other than—my own dear mother?"

Tears began to well in my eyes as I turned to face my ethereal lady guide. "Yes, dear Maestro. I instinctively knew that. I felt that connection in my heart."

The composer then nodded, as if he was satisfied with my response. "As you are so interested about her and my music then, yes, I admit that despite the physical loss of my mother, I had always felt her spiritual figure was always present, always guiding me when I would get restless with music ringing all the time in my head, seemingly making no sense at all. But, alas, my dear mother has taught me well. She has embodied the true meaning of Guardian Angel."

Suddenly Scriabin's figure appeared misty to me, and soon I could see him slowly vanishing under a heap of clouds, waving his hands.

I felt lighter and saw that I was floating too.

For the last time I tried to call out to the great composer, relaying to him the legacy he was leaving behind so he would always know he made a mark in the world.

"Maestro," I said. "Nemtin's universe—a speculative completion of Scriabin's *Mysterium*—and your *Seventh Piano Sonata* played by John Bell was recorded in a CD and carried by two persons, Mark and Carlos, up in the summit of one of the most beautiful peaks of the Himalayas. They risked their lives to get there to this unnamed and unclimbed peak. There they set free the spirit of your music, high above the clouds, and released your vision, your incredible energy and remarkable creativity into the majestic winds of high Himalayas . . . where you will live forever."

As Scriabin's figure slowly dissipated, he waved once more, mouthing the words. "I hear you and I thank you . . ."

His last word "you" reverberated as an overture began playing from one mountain peak to another. My friend, the lady whom I followed, began looking like a shadow, confirming what I had suspected all along—that she was indeed the equally talented mother of the great Russian composer who was taken too soon from this earthly realm only to continue to guide her son through the spiritual realm. I shall carry the spirit of Lyubov Petrova always in my heart and, to this day, I can still hear her voice, guiding me, like she guided her beloved son:

> Your mind is like a clear blue lake and your thoughts are the creative energy you can create so that whatever you want to create, you have the power to decide whether it is real or not real. Whatever you choose, the choice will lead you to the path of reality or the other side of it. This is the beauty of artistry. And creativity knows no bounds.

So as I looked up at the heavens, I bowed in reverence to my own creative Guardian Angel.

"Mother Lyubov, I am amazed with your talent, what you did in your time in such a short span of your life in our earthly world. I am honored and blessed to know you. However, I have but one question: why did it take you so long to be with your dear son? Aren't you both in the same dimension now?"

His mother's spirit replied with a smile as her figure floated above me, slowly dissipating in a soft cloud. "Dear child, I have always been guiding my son from my celestial home," I heard her distinct, clear voice. "But I wanted Sasha to know firsthand how his music has affected all those who love his music and appreciate his talents, especially those interested in his mysticism. That is why I guided you to him to show you how wonderful that part of his music was floating around the peaks of the

Himalayas—his dream partly fulfilled, but satisfying nonetheless."

Then she was one with the clouds, her orange dress spread across the sky like a fiery amber sunset glowing in the western horizon.

꧁꧁꧁

I moved my limbs to see whether I was alive and found myself in my bedroom. Had all this been but a dream?

Through the window I could see the sun was shining. I could hear the faint sound of one of Scriabin's piano sonatas serenading me awake as the pine trees were swaying with a gentle breeze. Mount Diablo peeped through the branches of the trees as the blue jays were busy chirping on a birch tree. The squirrels ran fast to hide the nuts. The wind chimes started echoing the tunes of high mountains from a faraway land and welcomed me back to my world.

It was about time to embrace a new day.

The Vigilant Muse

There are several pine trees that stand where my moderate-sized deck ends and I like to look at them. One in particular I could reach and touch. This tree stands tall, as if it could touch the sky. The autumn morning dew hangs like pearls, ready to drop. A little bird hops from one twig to another. Two squirrels start to chase each other around the trunk as another joins and looks at me with an expression as if wondering why I am there. As misty rays of sun weave through the branches, peering through the dense needles one can see the hazy landscape as Mount Diablo, the Devil Mountain, with greenish hue peeps its hilly head. A gentle cool breeze with a refreshing pine smell touches my face. This is the kind of morning that blesses my daily ritual of meditation and prayer.

After the morning ritual, I sit down at my breakfast corner with my little cockatiel, Samrat, who likes to nibble his seeds and millet as he merrily chirps away his incomprehensible chattering, which slows down at times with a birdie phrase, "Love you!"

My eyes scan through the window to find my favorite pine tree. The sun is up but it's still hazy and the pine tree looks wet with last night's rain. It looks very handsome, with its dark wet brown trunk and fresh green needles.

The pine tree whispers to the oak tree, "I like to talk to the two-legged creature who lives here who seems to know I keep my eyes constantly on her house. I think she's interested in me."

"Hello, what is going on? Are you in love?" asks the oak tree. "It's not possible simply because we are what we are."

"I know we are trees," snaps the pine. "I don't understand. We're all living beings. My love for the creature—the human is pure. We are beings with senses. I can feel the warmth as she wraps her arms around my trunk and I can smell her fresh scent."

"No doubt it is the scent of pine that rubs up on her," the oak tree huffs. "I see there is something between you and her. It seems you have forgotten your own brethren."

"You know that I care for you my dear oak tree," says the pine. "We grew up together and you shall always be by my side through sunny days and stormy nights. That will never change. Our brethren have been known to endure for hundreds, even thousands of years."

The pine tree continues to relate how the squirrels jump from her branches to the pine trees.

"You are ticklish as you laugh and sway and the squirrels get the message and run away," said the oak tree. "They eat the pine nuts from my cone then rest on my branches which is pleasant. The birds arrive to perch on your branches and mine and as they sing, their songs fill the air and then, you and I hum songs together with the birds as other trees join us with their music that composes the symphony of the trees."

"We stand tall together to protect her and her house," said the pine tree. "It is a nurturing kind of love."

ॐॐॐ

I'm dashing down the freeway after a long day at the Children's Hospital where I work. The late commute grinds my car to a stop-and-go pace as it battles through the piles of cars through the Caldecott Tunnel. I breathe easily as the thought of home and my backyard and the comfort of my favorite pine tree melts my tension away.

Finally, I am home. The sound of my car, the mechanical wheel moving sound appears to be music to my bird's ears and makes my bird chipper with joy. As I open the cage, he jumps on my shoulder, happily pecks on my cheek and starts his birdie talk—his usual way of asking me about my day.

I put the kettle on to boil the water for tea. As the kettle boils the water, my eyes search for that pine tree, but duties and responsibilities abound and I have to cater to my birdie Samrat's needs. At the moment, the cockatiel with its silver wings, dark silver feathers and crest on his head that flares when he's excited, has my undivided attention.

It's adorable how he says a few words like "I love you" and sometimes "toot" which I think means "good."

Nibbling pieces of cracker, Samrat screams "Night Night," and soon it's his bedtime. After placing him in his cage, I go out to the patio, sipping the steaming cup of tea, and look at the tree. The squirrels are quiet now, some are munching my hibiscus leaves and some are lying flat on their tummy on a branch. The birds are gathered in different branches resting and chirping before they go to their own sacred spaces to tuck in during the night.

The live oak sways with evergreen leaves and I don't think I'm imagining things when the tree whispers to me.

"Can you hear me?"

Stunned for a few seconds, I look around. "Yes I think I can."

"Did you know that the tall pine tree adores you?"

"He does! I like him very much."

"I shall tell him you feel the same then."

"Wait! I admire the tree for its beauty."

The oak tree eyes me curiously. "Are you sure it's nothing more?"

I shake my head, not knowing what was happening to me. Why am I talking to a tree? Is there some type of magic in effect? "I do not know what's real or not."

"Oh come now! You two-legged creatures, you humans are always problematic—wallowing in your bubble of self-indulgence."

I am dumbfounded. "What you mean?"

"I mean more than I said. Try to open your eyes to the world, there are sounds, colors and feeling which are all around us. The world just doesn't revolve around you."

"Please don't call me two legged. That's not nice. My name is Maya." I don't like being misunderstood or judged—even by a thing of nature. "Please tell the pine tree I wish to have a word with him."

The oak tree sways to one side, as if ignoring me. "Tell him yourself."

� � �

The pine tree stands tall, looking towards the sky as if there is some news from there it expects to receive. I start talking rapidly.

"Will it rain again? Will the pine branches sway?

"Yes," he whispers.

Last night it was so stormy that I worried about my tree friend. "I saw you were whistling with the wind and the wind chime was in concert with you. It was like a lullabye," I say. "I was afraid that you would be hurt by the storm. I'm so glad you are alright. You are so brave and strong that not even a twig has broken. You are so kind and giving to all of us, providing a place for the birds to chat and rest, for the squirrels to run around, giving them a place to rest. And as for me, I am grateful to you for protecting my house from the sun and wind."

I think I hear the oak tree start whispering again.

"In the evening when the moon comes out through the cloud and Mount Diablo sleeps, you should come out and whisper a tune. In that peaceful moment you will hear his bass voice," the oak tree said.

"So how can I tell whose voice is it is?" I asked.

"Mine is high pitched and the pine tree's voice is peaceful and meditative, even solemn."

For some reason, the mood suddenly became solemn for reasons beyond my comprehension.

I have to go. I will come out again in the evening. I want to be with you when the moon is rising and again before I retire. These are the words I long to share with my tree friend. But, alas, they are words I keep to myself.

The sky in the evening is reddish, resulting in a red moon. I see through the branches of the tree, as the moon plays hide and seek. Moonlight scattering over the pine tree makes it very dreamy. I recollect the day's events and believe that my rituals of daily life and my muse has merged and fused together. I cannot separate them as the muse is my ritual also, and I have to be with it ritualistically, to inspire me and relieve my tiring routine of life.

The moon comes out of the clouds, happily shining over the pine tree.

I am out in my patio again. The tree looks regal as the moonlight brushes the pine tree with silvery gray.

"Something tells me you wish to talk," I tell the pine tree, which sways as I feel a vibration.

Suddenly I hear a hum and then a deep voice as if it is coming from the depth of the ocean. It's the baritone voice of the pine tree.

"Yes," the pine tree replies, calmly and for a moment, he regards me almost as if he and I are equals. "There are number of things I want to talk with you about. First of all, I want to thank you for your love for us, I mean our kind."

"Of course, without 'your kind' we would not survive," I say.

The pine tree sways. "Some humans do not understand that what they are doing, cutting down the trees and building and building bigger mansions whether they need it or not is destroying not only our brethren but the planet."

The pine tree continues his diatribe. "Humans keep filling up all the hilltops and meadows with houses and hideous square box-like structures of tall living quarters. It's repulsive."

"I understand your frustration but people need places to live," I sigh.

Pine tree suddenly moves its branches strongly. I can feel the tree's agitation.

"That does not mean you chop all the forests around and build square boxes which sometimes end up empty as people cannot afford to stay there," he spews. "Trees plants, animals and humans benefit from each other. When humans and animals breathe they take oxygen and give off carbon dioxide. This carbon dioxide is taken up by plants and oxygen is given off in presence of sunlight in the form of photosynthesis during the daytime. So you see, we need each other. You may understand, but many humans have no respect for our kind and think they can do anything they want."

"Explain to me what they do to you," I say softly touching one of the branches.

The pine tree stiffens from my touch and I can't tell exactly how affected he is and in what way. He seems well aware of some people claiming to be tree-huggers. I have been one of them.

"Aside from cutting down my brethren, humans like to hang on branches and break them sometimes. It is vital to keep the branches intact, if you break them without sealing them, we're prone to acquire some kind of disease. Like humans, we are living creatures; it hurts and we also have the kind of heart that ails from these abuses. We have feelings that travel all over our bodies like you have nerves which travel through your body with your feelings and signals."

The pine tree pauses and I can feel the sad vibration as his branches sag.

"Just few days ago, a couple was engaged in a romantic embrace then suddenly something went wrong and before I knew it, they started hitting my trunk with their heavy backpacks, caused dents in my trunk and breaking a branch to release their anger."

I am appalled at the cruelty that my "own kind" can inflict. "I am so sorry they did that to you. Not all people are fully aware of the harm they cause on other living beings."

"Yes, I encountered another couple and they were nice as I heard them thinking of having a tree like myself somewhere in their yard when they settle down."

"So now you see how compassionate our people can be at times," I tell the tree.

The tree is silent which I hope means he is satisfied with my comment.

"Would you talk to me when I feel lonely?" I ask. "It makes me happy and peaceful when you and the oak tree keep me company."

"Yes," the pine tree says, "the other trees also like it when you go out to acknowledge them."

"I know you will hear them as you want to perceive all the senses around you," the tree continues. "You understand what it means to be one of us.

A gentle breeze makes the pine branches sway.

"Yes I will try to do that," I assure the pine tree. "You stand so tall as if you touch the sky during the day and at night I see when the moon comes out playfully through the clouds. Do you enjoy playing 'Peek-a-Boo' with the moon?"

"Yes I enjoy the moon's company at night," the pine tree replies. It is peaceful to have fun just the two of us."

"Can you see faraway lands from your vantage point?"

"I see whatever I could see being tall, but we get news from distant lands."

"Who brings it?"

"Why, the wind, of course."

I raise my eyebrows in surprise.

"Yes, the news travels as a gentle breeze at times and other times as angry storm," the pine tree adds. "The news is sometimes sad, such as reports of deforestation, and occasionally, it is joyful."

"How receptive is the wind and how do you communicate?" I know that the pine tree trusts me as he continues to share his knowledge about the hidden universe—hidden to human beings, that is."

"You have to feel the vibration of the universe in order to be receptive to communicating with other forms of nature," the pine tree explains, its branches moving. "Forests play a greater role in determining rainfall. Deforestation has already lowered the vapor flow significantly leading to reduced rainfall."

"I am glad people are getting to know these things," I remark. "My father used to share this knowledge with me when I was young but nobody paid any attention but me. He also told me you breathe out carbon dioxide at night."

"Yes he is right. In presence of sunlight, we make food for our body by photosynthesis. The process needs carbon dioxide, but at night that is stopped. So at night we inhale oxygen for the respiration, and carbon dioxide is a by product we exhale at night."

"It is so interesting to talk to you," I marvel to the tree. "Your voice is so deep—like the ocean and it lulls me to sleep."

"Then my dear, you must go to bed," he says. "I will also rest and rise tomorrow when the sun spreads its alchemy to the eastern sky. Good night. Sweet dreams."

☙☙☙

I ask myself what is this pure love—an abstract entity, eternal, primeval, everlasting? Love is not limited only between human beings. Love is expansive and all-inclusive—an energy that binds every form in the universe. It is then that I realize that my muse isn't just my beloved pine tree, but also his oak tree friend, the mighty wind and all forces of nature. The muse invigorates my morning thoughts and fulfills my evening dreams.

The branches of the pine tree sway. The dreamy moon peeps through the clouds, and at the distance, Mount Diablo, that crafty Devil Mountain, laughs at me, teasing as I utter everlasting words of serenity.

The wind chime sings while the gentle breeze through my muse sends me to a land beyond a land—the land of my dreams.

The Daring Escape

A dawn in 1606 slowly gave way to an early morning in summer. The sun's first kiss of the day imbued a red hue over the University of Padua in Italy.

The classic-style buildings stood majestic along the Bacchigione River and Brenta. The reflection of early sun on the blue water fragmented in pieces and then merged far away with dancing ripples. The blue sky softly shone down on the red-tiled rooftops where a few seagulls gathered. Along the blue waterfront elegant white marble statues greeted the passersby.

Padua, the famous university, center of early humanist research, was under Venetian rule at that time. At the triangular side of the plaza, five spirited young men were waiting for their teacher who would take them around to be oriented in the vicinity of Padua and Venice. Among the five, two came from England and other three were Italian. That was the way it was grouped, to encourage an exchange of their cultures and opinions and to develop a unique friendship among them.

All five young gentlemen dressed their best as all were wearing breeches cut below the knee and slightly puffed at the end. Two of them wore off-white loose white silk shirts accentuated with brown vests, while another wore a light cream shirt and beige vest. The other two wore gray breeches with loose silk shirts gathered at the cuffs and small ruffles with gold-colored buttons at the front. Crimson vests completed their ensembles.

The gentle summer breeze blew through their neatly-parted hair as the rhythmic sound of gondolas and barges passed along the waterways. The smell of red oleander and the sweet smell of wisteria from a hanging vine wafted in the air. All five young men gathered in front of a statue and began to introduce themselves, when a figure appeared at the other end of the plaza. They all could feel the presence of the figure and realized this was the teacher they were waiting for.

The teacher was of average build, with black hair neatly combed at the back above his shoulders. His triangular face was freckled, with a prominent nose, trimmed moustache and luminous, shiny brown eyes. He was wearing light brown breeches cut and puffed below the knees, a light blue silk shirt with ruffles at both wrists with gold studs at the front of his shirt and a light brown vest. He donned a silken hat with an upturned brim held in front with a decorative brooch.

"*Buona giornata*, young men," said the teacher, who introduced himself as Professor Luigi Giacomtti. "*Piacere di consoserti.*" It's nice to see you," he said, shaking each young man's hand. "We are standing in front of the Palazzo Del Bo which is the main university building."

Professor Luigi, who was department chair of rhetoric and one of the popular teachers on campus, took the students around in batches for the tour of Padua and Venice. He began to give them a short lecture on the history of the current events around the world as well as in Venice and Padua beginning with the High Renaissance period.

"This was and is a nexus of intellectual, scientific and artistic development. The period of Renaissance started in 1430. After 1450, the spirit of discovery gained momentum. Among the inventions were the printing press and gunpowder, which brought an end to armored knights and walled towns. Above all, there was the rediscovery of the writers and philosophers of classical Greece and Rome—Aristotle, Plato, Homer."

Professor Luigi asked the group if anyone knew the meaning of the term Renaissance. Robert raised his hand and said, "That means rebirth."

"Good," Professor Luigi said. "Robert, please tell us something about yourself."

"Robert Dudley from Surrey England," the boy bowed before the group. "I was in Oxford studying human anatomy, mathematics and literature, especially Shakespearean drama. I came here to study medicine."

A young enthusiastic man of average height and weight, Robert had light brown hair and a freckled face. It appeared that he was trying to grasp and absorb everything with his huge brown eyes.

Professor Luigi enlightened the group with his knowledge of humanism, which involved the time when Copernicus removed earth from the center of the universe and let humanity sail in the vastness of space.

"The new understanding of classical nudes and the science of perspective in painting made convincing illusions," Professor Luigi said. "In music, the High Renaissance saw polyphony. In spirituality, Martin Luther broke the monopoly of the Catholic Church and began the Protestant Reformation with an individual responsibility to God.

"Shakespeare examined the passion of humanity with timeless wisdom and incomparable poetry. We are now in 1606. We are still in the tender years of the new century," Professor Luigi continued, as the students drew closer, captivated by his lecture. "When this university was founded in 1222, the first subjects to be taught were law and theology. Anyone in the group studying theology?"

Allasandro of Pisa raised his hand.

The Professor nodded and continued. "The university expanded rapidly and the institution was divided in two—*universitas Iuristarum* for civil and canon law and *universitas artistarum* which taught astronomy, dialectic, philosophy, grammar, medicine and rhetoric. The student body was also divided into two groups—one for Italian students and the other for those who came from beyond the Alps. Since the 15th century, the university was renowned for its research in the areas of medicine, astronomy, philosophy and law. Anyone in the group studying astronomy?"

William Radcliff came forward. "I am from Middlesex England and plan to study mathematics and astronomy under the supervision of maestro Galileo."

"Splendid." Everyone's riveted gaze turned toward William, a tall young student with hazel eyes and light reddish brown hair. The group would later come to know of his very focused and serious demeanor.

Professor Luigi turned toward Carlo and Alleghero. "What about you two?"

"I am from Venice and come from a merchant family," replied Alleghero. "I want to study civil and cannon law and also dialectic."

"And I want to study civil law and philosophy," said Carlo, who also hailed from Pisa. "My family is well known for buildings. My ancestors were called upon by Queen Elizabeth to build fortified walls in England."

Professor Luigi credited the generosity and protection on the part of Venice, which enabled the University of Padua to maintain some independence from the Roman Catholic Church. The university adopted the Latin motto: "Paduan freedom is universal."

"The botanical garden of Padua, established in 1545, was one of the most beautiful gardens in world," Professor Luigi explained. "It was a place where the students from the university gathered to socialize and discuss their point of view. It is my hope that you all will do the same and enjoy doing so."

There were several museums including one that featured the history of physics, he revealed.

"This one is very popular among the students of Padua," continued Professor Luigi. "The museums garner visitors and students from around the world. Before I leave you on your own to visit Venice at your leisure, I have to tell you about the Navigilo Del Brenta, a canal which links Padua and Venice. It is a very pleasant sight to see several boats running along this canal singing and playing their flutes in a joyous mood. The calm stretch of waterways has a natural origin; the Venetian constructers diverted the main course of the canal to the south of the lagoon to prevent silting. The canal is managed by water locks, which can be opened and closed. Through this canal, students in their leisure time can ride to Venice where there are shops selling food, flowers, clothing, jewelry, books and more."

"In the mid-15th century, the Venetians turned their attention to the mainland expanding it from the inland. A rich family acquired the farmland and began building villas. These were used to oversee the agriculture states but soon became summer residences." Professor Luigi sighed. "All right young men, go have fun in Venice, behave, and come back in time to check your schedule on campus. I bid you goodbye. You will be taken care of by your individual departmental teachers, so all the best on your future endeavors and wishing you smooth sailing through your stay at the University of Padua."

Several boats were riding through this canal way to Venice; some were coming back to Padua. The narrow decorated gondolas rode through the canals in their leisurely rhythm. The gondolas were less in number than other boats like Battella or Carolinas. People from one passing boat would cheer to each other.

The students from Padua came in such a boat. Each student had his own desire to be fulfilled in Venice—away from his or her rigorous routine in Padua. At a distance from the Grand Canal, one could see the merchant ships blowing their horns and sailing away to a faraway land. Some had just docked, as others got ready for the voyage.

In Venice, there was the big open courtyard or piazza as far as the eye could see where people were strolling, chatting, singing and buying and selling things from the vendors. Around the large piazza, ladies with long dresses and lacy blouses and decorated hats were gliding gracefully. Their powdered faces were accentuated with loosely draped flowered lacy scarves. Their elaborate jeweled hair ornaments crowned their carefully curled locks and on some, crowned buns were made with their long hair.

The mansions sat on either sides of Grand Canal where the wealthy lived. There were narrow canals, which branched around Venice. The cozy mansions with their hanging balconies were accentuated with hanging flowering plants. They could be seen on either side of a narrow canal as the plants drooped to reach the water of the canal, the rainbow of colors swaying gently to greet the boats that came close, where young ladies were waving and greeting the passersby. The students from Padua in Professor Luigi's group were riding on two of those hired boats that came to Venice.

William, who was studying mathematics and astronomy, and Robert, who was studying medicine, were both thrilled to be in the intellectual hub that was Padua. Robert was very happy that he was in the institution where Andreas Visalias held the department chair of surgery and anatomy. Widely famous, Visalias published his anatomical discoveries in *De Humani Corpories Fabrice*.

Feeling lucky to be introduced with Carlo, Allasandro and Alleghero, the group of students quickly bonded with each other. It was as if they had known each other for a long time. Their excitement was palpable. They broadened their horizons by studying art, literature and music in addition to their own focus of study. They could foresee possibilities to discuss with each other what they were learning individually. They planned to come to Venice to relax as well as buy books and other study material. They were particularly interested in books that were banned at that time, such as the *Bible of Martin Luther*.

Young intellectuals such as these gentlemen also knew the benefit of social time and thus were eager to meet the pretty girls Amadora, Assunta and Angela, who was Alleghero's sister. Two of the girls were studying painting while the other was studying music.

They all went to a roadside restaurant where they consumed cooked fresh fish from the coast and oven-fresh bread as they enjoyed chatting and discussing different topics and exchanging new ideas. Before long, the students had to head back to their destination.

They were determined to pour their hearts out but there were so many thoughts and ideas that they were afraid would collide from the overflowing of opinions. There were so many things to be said in such a short time.

Angela, who liked Robert, wanted to know more about him and wanted to be close to him even though this was only the second time they had met. She looked at her brother Alleghero meaningfully to get his consent.

As if on cue, Robert suddenly approached Angela. "I am so please to be with you. Your voice is so beautiful and you have a charming personality." They held hands for few seconds as Robert made a courteous bow.

Angela blushed and managed to say, "I am very pleased to see you."

Meantime, William and Amadora stood very close together.

"Amadora I hope to see you soon. Please explain how you make the perfect chiaroscuro," William requested.

"Well then, William, you will have to explain to me the theory of planetary motions—what you are learning from your maestro Galileo," Amadora said, blushing.

"Certainly, Amadora," William said, his eyes glowing. "I am pleased to share whatever knowledge I have from the lectures. I am honored by your interest."

Then the young couple continued admiring each other with unspoken words.

Alleghero and Assunta knew each other from their childhood when they were playmates. Alleghero kissed Assunta's hand, bidding farewell.

Carlo and Allasandro encouraged the group to head back. "We shall give some money to Pietro who is waiting to take us back. I hope he will hide the books somewhere in his boat."

They parted with the young ladies who went back to their destination and the young men boarded the boat. During their boat ride, the tired young men reflected on their pleasant memories of the day as the last rays of the setting sun colored the ripples of the canal.

As the curtain of dusk fell on the waterways diffusing lights from the balcony of the mansions and playing hide and seek with the shadow of darkness, above the horizon one by one, the stars started to gaze down to the earth. Only the lulling sound of water thrust by the oars broke the silence of the darkness. Finally, the students arrived at Padua, each one managing to hide their books as they snuck back inside the campus after tipping Pietro generously.

Carlo and Alleghero studied law, while Allassandro tackled theology, as the rigorous learning process in Padua continued. Whenever they had time they would meet at the museum, as it was close by, where they would discuss the trials and tribulations of the process of their learning.

On occasion, they would go to the botanical garden of Padua and spend time sitting quietly on the white marble benches. William often went there and would pick up a fallen twig or take an ink pen and work on an equation on the ground exposed between the flowerbeds to solve a mathematical problem. He was very pleased that maestro Galileo took a keen interest in him and was looking for an opportunity to ask the maestro if he was interested in working with him in a particular area. So after initial hesitation he said, "Maestro, I would very much like to work on the project of 'New Stars and Planetary Movements,' " William said.

"Yes, William, you worked hard on the parabolic path of the projectile," Galileo responded. "You can surely work on my project."

William was very excited and wanted to tell the rest of his friends. Surely, he wanted tell his special sweet friend, Amadora. He kept on thinking that he would call on them at the museum, then reconsidered. "No, I will tell them in the botanical garden," he said to himself.

The garden was founded upon the deliberation of the senate of the Venetian Republic. A year after the inauguration in 1545, the botanical garden was used as a teaching facility. The garden was devoted to the growth of medicinal plants, those that produced natural remedies. The circular wall enclosure was built to protect the garden from night thefts, which occurred in spite of severe penalties.

William was fascinated by the layout of the botanical garden, the example of the medieval *Horti Conclusi* (enclosed gardens), making the architecture a perfect pattern of a square within a circle. It was the world's first botanical garden with a circular central plot, symbolizing the world surrounded by a ring of water.

William kept on thinking where they could get together. "The botanical garden is 22,000 square meters and every section is unique with exotic flowering plants, trees, intricate flower beds, some in the shape of sundials, as well as so many fountains."

He ultimately decided to ask everybody to meet at the principal palace, which was enriched with many fountains fed by a gigantic wheel hydrophore to ensure proper irrigation.

Robert, Carlos, Allasandro, Angela, Alleghero, Asunta and Amadora, all arrived one by one. They were all very excited and eager to know what news William was going to reveal. William was very excited, too.

"I cannot believe maestro Galileo has given me permission to join him in the study of 'New Stars and Planetary Movement," said William, taking a seat near a fountain.

The young people cheered and hugged each other. Amadora suggested that they should celebrate the occasion in Venice at the restaurant where they had first met.

Robert eagerly approached Angela. "I also have something to share."

"What is it?" Angela eagerly asked.

"It is not as great as William's news, but one of my anatomy dissections will be exhibited in the anatomy museum."

"Oh, that's wonderful news, Robert," Angela gushed. "We have to celebrate."

Carlos ambled toward William eagerly. "I've been meaning to ask you for some time now as to why maestro Galileo took all the credit for the discovery of the telescope. A Dutchman actually made the telescope, but Galileo was the one who first presented it in Venice."

William scratched his head and furrowed his eyebrows. "You are right, but the Dutchman's telescope had limited scope to scan the sky for new stars or planetary motion. Maestro Galileo redesigned it and made it powerful with stronger and powerful lenses."

"Maestro favors Archimedes and his principle more than Aristotle, is that right?" Robert inquired.

"Yes, he does," William answered.

Robert announced a plan to celebrate with the group in Venice—a suggestion that was met with a resounding cheer from everyone present.

৯৯৯

The students of Padua came to know that there was a struggle going on between Papal interdict and Venetian rights.

Paolo Sarpi, who was renowned for his learning and was appointed official counselor to the senate, drafted the Republic's reply to the Pope's draft. Paolo Sarpi's learning extended beyond his spirituality. The whole cast of his mind seemed to be scientific rather than philosophical.

As an anatomist, he had been credited with the discovery of the circulation of the human body a quarter of century before Harvey. He also discovered the valve in veins. As an optician, he earned the gratitude of Galileo himself, who acknowledged *mio padre e maestro Sarpi's* help in the construction of his telescope.

Carlo came to know about Sarpi's appointment as a counselor to the senate. It was late evening as he gathered the others. All five of them came out of their living quarters to a secluded place and started talking, anxious to know the outcome.

"The University of Padua should be above all this," said Alleghero. "The University's motto is to be free from papal interdict."

Allasandro had to intervene. "He is trying to excommunicate Venice and we are going to be in trouble."

Their murmurs rose above the harmony of the crickets and in the distance a ship blew a distress signal as the darkness of the evening fell. At that point, a night guard arrived to check on them.

"What is going on, why you are here in this hour of night?" asked the guard.

"We were exhausted after studying hard so we came out to stroll and to have fresh air so that we could sleep," the group replied.

The students of Padua soon got the news that Sarpi replied to the first brief of the Pope that the temporal matters were not within the jurisdiction of the Pope. The group of five and the three lovely ladies Amadora, Asunta and Angela started talking about the news. In spite of the Pope's threat of excommunication, Venice would ignore and dismiss Papal Nuncio with Sarpi's help with the following words: "It is nothing to us. Think now where the resolution will lead, if our example is to be followed by others."

On Sarpi's advice, the Doge (who would be worthy of the nation and acceptable to the people) banished all the Jesuits whose Spanish orientation had led them to take the papalist line.

Amadora and Asunta asked Carlo, "Why do we have to worry about all this? We came here for an education."

"We have to know what is going on around us, that is also education," Carlo replied. "Moreover, it matters to us very much that we are getting our education which is broad and open without Papal intervention. The church is trying hard to ban the books, which contradicts Padua's motto. It is the Papal monopoly. Why are they doing this? We should have the opportunity to read those books and figure out for ourselves what is right or wrong. People come here from all over the world to study. Do you think anybody will be willing to come if we have a narrow vision? It is very important that we know that we are a Venetian republic. If Venice loses her power and falls, then we Paduans, fall too."

Allasandro and Carlo were happy to find that Paolo Sarpi remained at the center of the stage, writing countless letters and polemics, preaching, disputing and debating, striving to more clearly define the celestial path of church and the terrestrial path of temporal princes.

Allasandro told the group that Sarpi achieved the name and fame, here and abroad and, to some, he was an Archangel, while to others, he was the Anti-Christ. People of Venice prostrated themselves to kiss his feet.

England and Holland openly wanted to help the situation. Finally, in April 1607, the Pope lifted the interdict. Anxiety remained, which hovered over Venice and Padua, that the Pope might try to impose his authority by force of arms with Spain as his willing ally.

ॐॐॐ

In Venice there was an influx of people from outside Italy, as she was very popular for her flourishing culture and education.

The Spanish population grew. The people of Venice observed an increase in number of Spanish people's gatherings in cafes and street corners. They observed that these people were possibly engaged in spying as the crime rate rose and people lived in panic and anxiety not knowing who would be the next victim.

In the fourth year in Padua for the group of five students, the mood of these students changed due to the changes of the political air around them. They were still working hard on their projects and were very close and friendly to each other. Their bond tightened as if they were all one unit. Unknown persons followed some of them when they were buying books or chatting at a roadside café.

One evening, Allasandro gathered the others, as their close group was very sad and serious about something. He came to know that Giovanni, a former student of theology from Padua, was in trouble. He was working as an assistant clergy in a small town close to Padua. In a weekly discussion, his comments about the individual responsibility to God seemed to bother other clergies.

Giovanni was very close to this group of students. He used to spend time looking after whatever their needs may be. At times he would take them home to meet his parents, who also became very close to these students.

It was initially reported that Giovanni had been thrown out of the clergy. If the Inquisition Committee decided to do that, then, who knew what might happen? They might put him in prison.

"They might drag him and drown him to death, as had been done to others in the past," Allasandro reported. "As fate would have it, they did not burn this unfortunate fellow as there will be questioning and an inquiry that would result in public condemnation; so secretly one evening, they took this prisoner by boat and put him in a cage and drowned him in the river by putting two heavy stones on each side."

The chilling story was a cautionary tale for the students who, every now and then, were harassed by the authorities and questioned on the kinds of activities they performed when they went to Venice. They were once followed in Venice as they were about to buy some books on religion, but managed to avoid a confrontation and retreat to a safe place to eat.

William was one of the students working with Galileo. The astronomical discoveries Galileo made with his telescopes were published in Venice in May 1610. There was a demonstration of Galileo's telescopes at the Venetian senate and Galileo gave sole rights for manufacturing them to the Venetian senate. The senate was very impressed at first and raised his salary; but later realized that the right to manufacture the telescope Galileo had given them was worthless and froze his salary.

He succeeded in impressing the Cosimo de Medici and Grand Duke of Tuscany. In June 1610, soon after publishing his famous book *Starry Messenger*, Galileo resigned from his post at Padua. He became chief mathematician at the University of Pisa and mathematician and philosopher to the Grand Duke of Tuscany.

As a student of Galileo, William was in an uncomfortable situation and his work was related with the movements of the moons of Jupiter and the contents of *Starry Messenger* were his guide and inspiration. The *Starry Messenger* was not welcomed by the Venetian senate. After Galileo resigned at Padua, William communicated with Galileo.

It was difficult and time consuming during 1610 and thereafter to communicate with a person who lived in other towns. Above all, Galileo's book was not welcome by the authorities of Padua University, as the Venetian senate was not happy with Galileo.

The motto "Paduan freedom is universal," was shaky and the students of Padua were confused and bewildered. William wanted to meet Galileo in Pisa secretly and wanted to thank him. He arranged to go to Pisa by horse-drawn cart, hiding under a stack of hay. After a short visit with his professor and mentor, he left. While he was coming back he had to hide in a hole in the bed of the horse-drawn cart.

Before he left, his professor gave him a stack of equations that he could never publish. These equations and theories had to be hidden for fear of getting caught by the Inquisition Committee. William was brave enough to transport it as he was from England so somehow he could get this out of the country. There was a possibility that within another few weeks when the merchant ship of his uncle would dock near Venice. He could send the papers through him to another country.

As the horse-drawn cart rode up and down through a rough unpaved road, William's heart was speeding as fast as the horse raced through the dark. While it was drizzling, he could feel the cold breeze as he opened a door of the wooden platform. He put his head out of the hole for a little and gazed above, toward the horizon. The glow of the moon, which hid behind the clouds and the thin layer of fog made the landscape very mystical.

Beyond the thin foggy curtain there was an outline of landscape. It felt like little more riding could help get near the landscape. But the landscape never drew nearer, it just lured you like a mirage and you just kept on riding. As he reflected where the path of his life might fall in that very moment, he felt very drained, as the prospect of his unfulfilled dreams and goals might disappear at any time.

At this moment he was planning to get back to Padua University without being noticed. It had been a long, tiring journey. The driver of the horse-drawn cart took pity on him and suggested that William get refreshed in his tiny cottage, which was pretty close to Padua.

He arrived in Padua early the next morning. It was easy for William to mingle with the crowd of students with out being noticed. He was determined that their group should plan an escape from Padua and travel as far as they could, away from the Venetian senate.

The day went by as usual, as he worked at the lab, studied, and finished his project. The calculations of the equations were stored in his head, but there were other things like charts and he thought of doing a smaller version with abbreviations.

The next thing on his mind was to get in touch with his beloved group of friends. They all agreed to meet at the botanical garden in their favorite place, an artificial cove made with big rocks and boulders, lined with beautiful flowering vines. Close by, there were man-made waterfalls that constantly murmured around the rocks.

It was late afternoon when they gathered after their day in the university was done. The young ladies Amadora, Assunta and Angela were present also. They started planning their way out from Padua and Venice. Allasandro pleaded for his friend Giovanni, he was really in deep trouble, he was sure to face the Inquisition Committee and he would be doomed. William asked Amadora to sketch a detailed plan that could be hidden in a landscape painting.

It was decided that Carlo and Robert would take one boat. Giovanni would be in the same boat, but hiding in a space around the bottom behind a plank. The floor of the space had a secret door which could be open to the water if this boat was caught, so Carlo and Robert could signal with a tapping sound and Giovanni could swim under the water until he was rescued.

The boat would ride up to a merchant ship that would dock soon beyond the Grand Canal. This was the same ship that belonged to William's uncle that had brought William and Robert to Venice. Robert had a plan to revisit the crew just to say hello.

William, Allasandro and Amadora would take a gondola to the merchant ship. William had the most danger and responsibility, as he would carry the unpublished documents from Galileo. The plan was that if they were caught, the gondolier who was working for Alleghero would hide it somewhere in the gondola.

Assunta, Angela and Alleghero would take a boat from the Gulf of Venice that would come out to the Adriatic Sea. Their plan was to tell the authorities that they were on their way to Greece for study and vacation.

At the coastline of the Adriatic and Ionian Sea, they would board a ship to Athens and meet the rest of the group at Izmir in Turkey where the ship that belonged to William's uncle would stop on the way to their final destination in England.

It was widely known that their group of young intellectuals was under observation of the authorities. The group understood that the plan had to be implemented perfectly in order to ensure their safety. They had no other option—they would have to leave their beloved university in Padua and also Venice.

The day arrived when everyone orchestrated their plan and boarded their boats in different locations. Carlo and Robert boarded their boat and Giovanni secretly got in the boat as well. They had traveled through the canals several times, while they were in Padua. This day felt so different, their hearts were beating faster with anxiety, the rhythm of the oars beating the water felt like a moaning soul and familiar landscapes with happy memories were running backwards, disappearing from them.

In front of them, they could see the outline of a boat. The boat slowed down, and a person waved at them to stop. Giovanni quickly exited from the bottom of the boat to the water, and hid near the rudder. They were all frozen with fear. After a few questions and safety checks, their boat was allowed to proceed. This part of their plan had worked. After the other boat could no longer be seen, Giovanni was fished out of the water.

In the gondola, William, Amadora and Allasandro were also en route. William kept Amadora and Allasandro hiding in a cabin, as in Venice they were questioned about their destination. Allasandro had to plunge in the water for few minutes. As Amadora stayed in the cabin, a person came to inspect the cabin so she hid herself in a large compartment, which had a lid. The gondolier put his utensils and a heavy lamp on the top so the person in charge did not bother to go in detailed inspection. William answered the questions the person asked and presented the permit he had saying that the ship belonged to his uncle.

The gondola started again, Allasandro was still somewhere beneath in the water. The gondolier pushed forward until the boat was beyond the reach of the person who was inspecting. Soon, the gondolier spotted Allasandro who was hanging on one side of gondola panting for breath. They boarded the ship and within a short time the ship blew its horn and started moving. The gondolier started singing his song as he bid the ship farewell. Carlo, Robert, Giovanni rushed to the deck to welcome William, Amadora and Allasandro. The young group sadly gazed at the shoreline of Venice as it slowly but surely disappeared into the vast horizon as if it were only but a dream.

The House by the Creek

Noyakhali, an idyllic town in the east part of undivided Bengal in India, lay in a fertile landscape surrounded by tall palm and coconut trees whispering in the gentle breeze. Above the land stretched a dome of blue sky that descended to kiss the golden paddy fields as river and creeks danced along side by side.

There were houses big and small nestled around the landscape where Hindus and Muslims lived happily sharing bonds and close ties with each other. The neighbors, who had mutual generosity and respect for each other, celebrated their festivals and religious rites without consequence.

The political landscape in 1946, when a storm of communal riots blew over the eastern part of Bengal and the western part of Punjab in India before India gained independence, told a different story. With the riots came a wave of terrorism that swept along with it both death and destruction.

Mahatma Gandhi arrived with a peace mission to Noyakhali feeling optimistic that his presence would have a calming effect. He visited the towns and villages in the area, section by section, daily treading unpaved and muddy paths. As always, Gandhi walked in front of his followers wearing his signature attire striding firmly with his walking stick.

One of the followers was a young journalist, Bimal, who on one such daily tour, accompanied Gandhi and his group down a narrow, muddy path, which led through the paddy fields and curved toward a pond where blossoming lilies' sweet fragrances scented the air.

A scorched granary sat desolate in the shade of the trees while the surrounding coconut trees sighed with the breeze. Nearby a charred house creaked in a blast of wind and a burnt smell filled the air as Gandhi passed by. The creaking sound of the burned house continued as if it wanted to be acknowledged.

Way past a turn in the road, a house that was not damaged but standing elegantly by the creek surrounded by lush greeneries featured all varieties of fruit trees like mangos, lychees, and jackfruit. There was also a vegetable garden and a medium-size pond for edible fish. The pink lilies that graced the pond seemed to have a story to tell.

The wooden carved door at the front of the house stood half open. An aura that surrounded the house affected the group of visitors with a feeling of uneasiness. The group stopped and looked at each other.

Gandhi turned to the young journalist in the group. "Bimal, is this the house?"

Bimal came forward, his head down. "Yes, *Bapujee*."

As the father of the nation, Gandhi was accustomed to being fondly called "Bapujee" by all Indians.

Gandhi motioned for Bimal to take the lead as it was the journalist's desire to see and write down every thing exactly "as it is no less or no more." As he entered the house, Bimal felt that it might have been recently occupied but that its occupants may have left in a hurry. The living room furniture was moved, a table was upside-down, and pieces of broken sculpture lay strewn on the floor. A painting on the wall was crooked, one lacy curtain was torn, and there were rust-colored footprints on the floor.

Bimal continued walking through the house along a hallway leading to the kitchen on one side and the bedrooms on the other. The smell of cooking spices still lingered in the air; one person from the group took a deep breath and said, "Someone must have been cooking here not too long ago."

Across the hallway were several bedrooms. Two of the medium-size bedroom closets were flung open and women's garments like saris of different designs and colors were strewn on the floor. Petticoats designed to wear underneath a sari and blouses to match the saris were scattered across the floor and furniture. In one of the bedrooms, the pillows and bed sheets had been torn and lay in heaps over broken furniture and shattered photographs.

While Bimal was taking photos of this scene someone from the group called him from the master bedroom and Bimal ran to see what was going on. Before him lay a ghastly scene of splattered bloodstains on the walls and as well as the ceiling. Long streaks of dried out blood that stained the walls made his skin crawl. The carved wooden headboard of the bed bore a similar stain. The bed sheets were pulled from the bed, as were the pillows. Pieces of rope lay on the bed.

Controlling his emotion, Bimal summoned and guided Gandhi to the room.

"Bapujee, these are all blood-stained images." Bimal's voice echoed feelings of grief and despair. "I understand, people have drowned themselves in the sea of hatred and rage."

Gandhi shook his head sadly.

At that moment, a golden retriever ran into the room whimpering as it sat near Gandhi's feet, as if the dog knew who Gandhi was. The group was moved in tears by the devastation in the room even without knowing what had happened.

A man from the neighborhood then entered the room, knelt down at Gandhi's feet and started crying pitifully. He felt compelled to share what he witnessed but he was choking with fear and sadness. Bapujee assured the man he was safe now and encouraged him to tell his story.

"A day before yesterday around midnight, I heard a group of people shouting Allah's name," the man said, breathing heavily. "They were carrying fire torches and surrounded this house—the house of Sarkar Babu, my neighbor. Then, I heard awful noises as if the house was being invaded and broken into."

The man paused to wipe his eyes.

"Then I heard screams of a woman's voice and realized it was the lady of house calling for help. I've known Sarkar Babu and his family for a long time, but I felt helpless. I could not do anything."

The man said that according to Sarkar Babu's daughter, Nandini, who knocked on his door very early the next morning, there were several attackers armed with swords and bamboo sticks. "I am fearful even now and ask for help. If the attackers know that I speak to you now, they will harm me and my family. I am a Muslim. My name is Rahim. Sarkar Babu and his family have been close friends of mine for a long time."

He said that Nandini looked very pale and trembled uncontrollably from her ordeal. "Her clothes were wet and dripping with water. She told me that she hid herself in the pond and managed to survive by holding onto the moss and the lilies. Nandini cried out loud and said, 'The attacker's decapitated Baba (Father) in front of my Ma and started playing soccer using his head as a ball.' "

The man's body shook as he recalled Nandini's chilling account: "Ma screamed in terror until they stuffed torn pieces of cloth in her mouth and tied her with a rope. Then, she fainted. Thinking she was dead, the men carried her and threw her in the bushes, near the rice paddies. One of them started pulling my clothes off while another slapped me and yanked my hair. I kept screaming and my faithful dog, Bahadur jumped on the attackers and started to bite them. So the men tried to fight off Bahadur, trying to kill him but my dog ferociously attacked back. During the struggle, I escaped. I later heard my dog barking, so thankfully, he managed to also escape through a stairway to the roof. The dog saved my life."

Bimal shook his head as he listened to the man's story. "Rahim, where is the girl now and does anyone know what happened to the mother?"

Rahim cowered, as if he was afraid of being discovered by the attackers. "Bapujee, I am worried and scared to tell what else I know."

Bapujee took his hand and assured him that he and his group would try to help him as much as they could.

"Nandini begged me for help," Rahim continued. "So I went out with her to search for her mother in the rice paddies. Luckily, her mother was still alive, badly bruised, but thankfully, still alive. I carried the mother back to my home as Nandini followed. My wife, Shelma, gave them tea and dry clothes."

"I offered them shelter in my home and asked them to put on *burkas* to conceal their identity. They rested through the heat of the day. After midnight, I asked my friend who has a bullock cart to take them to our doctor's house where they could be safe for a short time. They boarded that cart hiding behind the load of rice bags and were taken to the safety of the doctor's home. Before leaving, Nandini asked if I could arrange passage for them to Calcutta. They had relatives who lived in the vicinity who would offer them a place to stay for now. Before Nandini left, she asked if I could take good care of her loyal dog, Bahadur, to whom she's grateful to for saving her life. I assured her that I would be honored. A hero like Bahadur deserves a good home."

Rahim paused briefly from recounting the tragic events that had befallen his neighbors. "Tell me, Bapujee, who started this? Why we are in misery? We used to live here peacefully and in harmony with each other."

Gandhi sighed as he placed his hand over Rahim's head. "We have to be strong together and stand firm against this senseless riot."

Gandhi called Nirmal, one of his loyal followers, to arrange a secure passage for Nandini and her mother to ensure their safe destination. Nirmal responded that he would arrange the medical supply truck to pick them up from where they were staying and take them to Ferry Ghat (the docking station) near the city of Dacca. There they would board an early ride by boat and then take a train directly to Calcutta.

"I will arrange for someone to accompany them to make sure they reach their destination safely," Nirmal said.

Rahim wanted to accompany Nirmal to see Nandini and her mother, Shobha Devi, whom he fondly referred to as *Bhabijee*, a term of endearment used to call an elder brother's wife, for the last time.

The next morning, while it was still dark, Rahim and the truck driver picked up Nandini and her mother. The stars still shone and the day was drawn with a pale light brush in the eastern sky. Under the crescent moon, a few birds began their early songs as they fluttered their wings.

As promised, the boat sat waiting in the water, carrying the hope for survival not just for Nandini and her mother but for future generations. Rahim bid farewell to his neighbors and friends and wished them a safe journey. Before their departure, Nandini once again made sure that Rahim would take good care of Bahadur. Nirmal said that he would do his best to send the dog with a medical supply person to Calcutta, perhaps later after Shobha Devi and Nandini have settled, if they wished. Despite their grief over losing the patriarch of their household, the women were overjoyed at the prospect of seeing their faithful dog, who had become a beloved member of their family.

Nandini and her mother got into the boat and soon it slowly moved away from shore as Rahim stood on the bank of the river watching them.

His figure grew even smaller with each stroke of the oars. Nandini and her mother, still wearing those all-concealing *burkas*, watched the sad, but relieved face of Rahim disappear in the distance.

Much later, when Nandini and Shobha Devi reached the train station, there were people waiting for them wearing Red Cross badges. One of them was a nurse. They boarded the train and were escorted to a compartment occupied by Red Cross workers.

The train whistled and pushed forward. The mother and daughter, despite their recent trauma, felt a magical protection around them as the train gathered speed and whizzed through countryside, leaving behind their once blissful home. They looked around them, at the nurse and other volunteers whose smiles warmed their hearts. Assured by their newfound safety net, Nandini and her mother removed the *burkas* and hugged each other tightly.

After wiping their tears of grief and relief, they turned to face the train windows as their hearts raced faster and faster with the uncertainty of the unknown. While still numb from their tragedy, they found comfort by holding hands. As the distance from their home grew greater, they cried out loud for the first time, but it would be a long time before they would find peace from their pain.

A House as Grand
as Great-Grandmother Roma

Kajari, who loved to spend time at her Grand-mother's house, was used to getting lots of attention from her Grandparents. They were her storytellers and her confidants.

The one person who intrigued Kajari the most was her Great-Grandmother Roma from her mother's side, who used to live with her own Grandparents.

Nine-year-old Kajari couldn't get enough of the old woman who managed to fascinate and charm Kajari with her elegant demeanor. There's an image Kajari has of Roma playing the clarinet in the evening in her room on the second floor of their grandiose house. A curved paved road led to the huge wooden door—the entrance to the house.

The year 1958 was a peaceful time in India—eleven years after India claimed its independence. In many ways, Roma's elegance ran parallel to the home where she lived. The stately house was but a small gem in the big city of Kolkata in west Bengal, India—a cosmopolitan city renowned for art, culture and literature.

The ground floor, India's version of the first floor, featured a covered wide mosaic corridor that greeted entrants. On the left side of the corridor was a courtyard.

On the right there were guest rooms as well as a living room and family room.

The house was blessed with staircases on either side of the corridor. Roma, dressed in her white sari, preferred to take the fancier staircase with its black and pink mosaic and wide steps, which curved upstairs leading to her room on the second floor.

Stepping into her room, there were large windows and a white marble floor bordered with black marble. Roma would scan her room to ensure that everything was neatly kept. This room had a wooden canopy bed with a mahogany-decorated headboard. Wooden poles at each corner of the bed were used to hang the mosquito net at night. The bed was always neatly made, with two big pillows with lacy covers. There was a ceiling fan and decorated lights on the walls.

An oval table with a marble top flanked by two wooden chairs on either side stood near a door, which led to a hanging balcony. The tabletop was always packed with books, journals and daily newspapers. After Roma's morning walk, she would take the daily newspaper and read some of the headlines as well as the editorial page. A bookcase with sliding doors was on one side of the room close to the oval table. The bookcase was packed with leather-bound books.

Bengali classics by notable literary artists as Bankim Chandra, and Rabidranath Tagore's songbooks and book of poems were all there for Roma's reading pleasure and at times, she would read a few poems aloud whether or not anyone was listening.

On the other side there was an armoire and a dresser with an oval mirror, which boasted a carved wooden frame and box-like compartments for storing things. If Roma expected a visitor, she would check her attire and hair in front of the mirror. Despite Roma's age, she always looked very elegant to Kajari.

Kajari would watch in fascination as Roma turned dressing into an art form. The elderly yet elegant woman would drape herself in a white golden-bordered sari and tie her long hair up in a bun. The sari used to drape her head was like the white sheer curtains that draped her windows. On the either side of her head were golden barrettes studded with precious stones to keep the sari in place.

Standing five-feet-four inches tall, with olive colored skin, a sharp nose, luminous black eyes and a regal smile, to nine-year-old Kajari, Roma resembled a sculpted figure—like a work of art herself. When she played the clarinet, the gold bangles on her right hand and diamond ring on her left ring finger dazzled with each movement.

The tinkling sounds of the bangles in the background fascinated Kajari as she would imagine an old castle and a beautiful, young princess delicately padding her tiny feet on a marble floor as tiny silver bells at her anklet created a melodious sound in the corridor. *She will make her appearance shortly,* Kajari thought with bated breath.

Being the oldest person from Kajari's maternal side of the family earned Roma the honor of fondly being called *"Bima."* Born in 1886, Roma was one of four daughters. Having finished her education at home, Roma was praised for her talent in music and writing. She had a special talent for writing poetry, which she used to recite in public and was awarded by renowned poets who lived at that period.

When Roma was sixteen she married Atul, a handsome young man of twenty-six, who finished law school and passed the Indian Civil Service Examination before he became a judge of the lower court. He then progressed to an even higher position later in life.

Of the several stories Kajari heard about Roma, one was her favorite. Roma used to be secretary of a women's organization, where women used to work on different handicrafts. The organization helped empower women by encouraging them to hone their talents and sell their crafts, which would provide money. In turn, this boosted their self-esteem.

Another story that Kajari heard concerned a young woman who used to help Roma clean the house. The young woman died while delivering her baby, as the woman never got any medical care. Frustrated by the system, a grief-stricken Roma aimed to do something, so she decided to train to be a midwife, specializing in childcare, to help the less fortunate people who lived in a shanty town. This act; however, was not welcomed by society, family and friends. Roma proceeded with her plan anyway and after her training she attended to the needy, advising them on how to take care of their babies and young children. Knowing this noble deed made Kajari love Roma even more.

Often, the little girl would watch as Roma sat close to the door, leading to the hanging balcony where she played some blissful tunes with her clarinet. These melodies at times made Kajari feel sad and other times, joyous.

"Bima, did my Great-Grandpa play his clarinet with you?"

"Yes, my dear child, he played very well and often," Roma replied, seeming pleased with Kajari's interest. "We often had private concerts at our home with our musician friends."

She continued her story. "Years ago, at the end of the day, when your Great-Grandfather, Atul, came home from court exhausted from his judiciary tasks, he would say 'Roma, let us have some tea.' Hema, your Grandmother, would come running upon hearing her father's voice. She would jump up on his lap and give him a huge hug, then Atul would continue the conversation about his day."

He would tell me, "Roma, I had a very exhausting day. It was a tough civil suit and lawyers from both sides just kept going on and on." I would try to take his mind off his stress and talk about music, so I would say, 'I want to let you know that I have arranged a dinner and musical event on Friday evening at our house. I informed all your musician friends to come and play. You should play your piece, too.' "

"And your Great-Grandfather would reply, 'Oh that is great! I will love to play a piece on my clarinet. What about you?' To which I responded, 'Yes, I will play something, but I have not decided yet.' "

Roma paused, eyeing Kajari as she continued to listen to her story. "We had friends who played other musical instruments who they played in a group together and individually in our house. The musical get-together became a monthly gathering."

There must still be so many things I don't know about my Great-Grandmother, Kajari thought. *She is indeed, a very special person and a very special Great-Grandmother.*

Later in life, Roma, who was a widow, lived with her only daughter, Hema, Kajari's maternal Grandmother. Roma's daily routine was interesting. She would get up early, perform her daily hygiene rituals, then dress up in her usual elegant attire. She would then call the gatekeeper to ask whether the chauffeur had arrived as she planned to go out for her morning ride around the bank of the Ganges.

Roma then asked Kajari, "Would you like to go one of these days?"

"I'd love to have a ride with you!" Kajari replied with excitement.

Kajari accompanied Roma several times whenever she visited her Grandma's house. For Kajari, the early morning rides were great fun, as she beheld the sights and sounds of the streets of Kolkata. Big hoses used to wash the streets made whooshing noises when water came rushing out. During this time, part of the city was just waking up; shopkeepers were preparing for their stores to open. The car they rode in used to pass the living quarters and go zigzagging and weaving through Park Circus and the Chowrangee area where there were shops and restaurants, then pass the Victoria Memorial, an imposing, huge marble building with a garden, built during British rule.

Inside the building housed artifacts from Queen Victoria's reign. Kajari and Roma used to take the road with avenues of big trees, then past a big open space with green grass, then they would be driven along a road leading to the bank of the Ganges. The car would stop and Roma and an excited Kajari would get out of the car and begin their leisurely walk. The river was full, bank to bank, and the fishermen were alongside their boats. There was a steamer, which suddenly whistled. The sun came out through a passing cloud and colored the river pinkish-red. The ripples touched with red, danced continuously. The cool breeze and the tranquility refreshed them completely and before long, it was time to return home.

"Shall we stop at Flurry's for some pastry and patties on the way home?" Roma asked Kajari, who beamed and said, "Yes!"

They came home with the goodies and in no time, after settling down a little after their excursion, Kajari started devouring the treats. Roma would have a bowl of *Muri* (puffed rice) with milk and a banana and a cup of tea. As the steam from the hot cup of tea swirled around, Kajari asked Roma to tell another enchanting story of her past.

Roma sat and ruminated over her cup of tea. She told of the time she organized a group of women to march at the town square where she lived. There they burned the clothes imported from a Manchester mill in England. The clothes from overseas overflowed the market, threatening the value of Indian goods, which were almost banned. The Indian weavers were tortured and there were places where the weavers' thumbs were amputated.

As the wife of a renowned judge, Roma had to undergo a lot of agony to organize this peaceful protest. She thought it was morally right to do so. The women of that locality gathered around and carried the national flag designed at that time.

Riveted by this latest story, Kajari asked, "How long ago was this, Bima?"

"Dates are not important right now for you will forget, but remember this is a true compelling story, my dear child," Roma answered taking a deep long breath. She continued.

She told Kajari that she took a huge risk leading the charge of women in the procession at the town square, remembering what it felt like to take part in the daring escapade as if it were only yesterday.

"British quit India! British quit India!" She remembered shouting along with the group. "Glory to mother India!"

They came to the town square peacefully as police followed them. They stopped at the town square and started burning the clothes from the Manchester Mills. British police randomly charged them with their batons, mounted police on horseback tried to disperse them. One after one, the women fell on the ground as blood from the injured stained the road.

Roma fell on the ground holding her national flag high. Despite all her agony she shouted, "British quit India! *Bande Mataram*!" She was rescued by the emergency medical services and so were the other women. Many peaceful protestors were incarcerated for a few months. The movement kept on going like a spark of wildfire from one town to another.

She stopped, took a deep breath as she transitioned back to present day. Kajari's eyes sparkled, envisioning this impassioned recount of a very emotional, historical event.

"That is all for today," declared an emotionally weary Roma.

Although Kajari was disappointed by her Great-Grandmother's sudden ending to her story, she had to ask, "Did my Great-Grandpa say anything about what you did?"

"Yes, he went to the hospital and took care of us and bailed us out from prison," Roma said. "He later congratulated me for my courage and praised me for protesting a cause that I believed was wrong."

Kajari looked outside. A tree was swaying with a gentle breeze as the blooming red flowers peeped through the branches. Kajari was startled, imagining Roma's bleeding wounds. She traveled back to that particular time and space, alarmed but proud to imagine "bleeding Great-Grandma." Kajari's heart started pounding with excitement to be honored as a great-grandchild of this courageous lady.

She reached out to Roma and hugged her.

"I'm so proud that you are my Great-Grand-mother," Kajari said, holding on tight. "I'm the luckiest girl in the world."

The Sensational Sunrise

On a clear crisp morning, Bithi and her little sister, Jimki, started their journey from Kolkata, a big city in West Bengal, India to Darljeeling with their mother and her group of friends. Darjeeling was a popular vacation spot, a picturesque town in the northern part of the state of Bengal at the foothills of the Himalayas. October in 1960 proved to be, more or less, a peaceful time—it had been thirteen years since India gained independence from the British.

Their mother Renuka planned to attend a conference where local senators from a different part of West Bengal were meeting with the chief minister of Bengal. There were several matters on the agenda, such as adult education, childcare and maternity. Renuka's involvement in several voluntary organizations garnered her an invitation to the conference.

Bithi, the older sister, was twelve and Jimki was seven. Both were very excited as they talked about their destination, telling their friends and cousins they were going to Darjeeling. They were proud to tell their teachers that their mother was attending the conference and would take them along with her. Their father accompanied them to the station to bid them goodbye. Soon they joined the others in the group that included senators and professors.

The group arrived a little early at the station to find the train was there ready for boarding. The moderate-sized compartment could accommodate six of them, a party of two children and four adults. The steam engine whistled, the wheels turned with a thug-thug-thug sound as the train started slowly then gradually reached its speed. Bithi and Jimki saw their father wave his handkerchief until his figure became smaller and smaller and he disappeared in the background.

The excited and happy sisters were the center of attention, providing a welcoming distraction for the adults as Renuka's friends all warmed up to Bithi and Jimki. One of them asked, "Are you going to be happy spending some time with us? We are thrilled you two young ones joined us. It's great to be able to catch up, as we don't often have time to chat as we're always in a rush. So we can talk about your school life, friends and other activities you're involved in."

The sisters were very happy the adults took so much interest in their lives, which included dance classes and sporting events.

"I'm really enjoying school because I have so many friends who also like to dance and play sports," said Bithi.

"My friends, Sucheta and Chitra, and our teacher Mrs. Folger made a dress for me that looks like a dahlia for a play we'll be in at school," Jimki said, excitedly.

"How wonderful," said Pratima, one of the educators.

Bithi loved the sound of the train as it swayed side to side. When the train's whistle blew, an excited Bithi exclaimed to her sister, "Oh, what fun! We are going to a mystery land." Once the train was on its merry way, the girls settled in with Jimki busy with her coloring book and Bithi writing in her diary.

The compartment of the train was exclusive and luxurious, with plenty of space between the sleeping bunks, and featured maroon cushioned seats, made of leather. Sheer lacy curtains on the windows were drawn with matching ropes. The bathroom door also had curtains and there was a shower and small area with a dresser for cosmetics.

"Dinner is going to be served in our compartment," Mother Renuka announced. Those words were music to Bithi's ears. A charming and neatly dressed man with a decorated turban appeared shortly and took their orders. Within half an hour dinner came.

The tables underneath the seats were pulled out and a white tablecloth, embroidered napkins, and silverware soon sparkled on the decorated tables. When they finished dinner, beds were made, and the sisters went to their allotted bunks to retire. The train sped through the dark night with a shrill whistle as if warning the dark night, "Here I come." Slowly, Bithi's and Jimki's eyes were getting heavier and heavier and they fell asleep.

A few peaceful hours rolled by until suddenly, Bithi heard some voices and it seemed the train was about to stop, kind of jerking on its way. Bithi and Jimki saw their mother pulling the chain hard to stop the train and, in that act she was almost suspended in air. It took a little while to understand that some intruders were trying to break into their compartment. In the meantime, Renuka's friends did all they could to prevent the robbers from coming inside the compartment.

One of the friends was holding a sugar cane stick that she had bought at the Howrah station where they started. She jokingly said then, "If needed, this will help to discipline somebody." She proceeded to use it to hit and poke one of the intruders.

Another friend took a dirty, smelly mop left by a train janitor by mistake and was placing it over face of another intruder.

Pratima, another friend, aimed the pointed heel of her shoe to hit the forehand of the robber who was tightly holding the window of the compartment as he tried to get in. Bithi saw Pratima's elegant ring dazzle with light as she lifted her hand to hit the intruder.

It was very amusing that the robbers were singing and rhyming in their language as they tried to gain entry. Bithi remembered hearing them sing: *The train is going thug, thug, thug / We will hug, hug and hug / Take the boxes one by one / And then we will run, run and run.*

Both sisters were shocked to see the pandemonium increase. Their fingers and toes were cold with fright. Jimki was holding Bithi tight and her eyes were wallowing in tears.

The train stopped and started whistling almost continuously. The police cars blew their sirens, a police officer and the guard came to the compartment and assured Renuka and her friends that they had captured two of the robbers, but one fled. The police officers promised they would stay on the train until it reached its destination.

They were safe. The incident had ended as suddenly as it started. Feeling reassured of their safety, Renuka and her friends hugged Bithi and Jimki assuring them that they were going to reach their destination soon and safely.

The train started and soon reached the next station, Shiliguri, a small town up on the mountain shrouded with pine trees. There they changed trains and took a narrow gauge train to Darjeeling station. The train began its ascent to a higher elevation. The train, turning and twisting like a snake, seemed like a toy as it climbed the mountain. It would go forward and then suddenly would push backward. Bithi and Jimki thought this first experience was quite fun.

The excited girls reached their hands out of the window of the train as if they could touch the remarkably unique landscape. The pines in the forest beamed a vivid green. Mountain ranges hovered above as if one could reach up and touch them, but then the mountains would retreat suddenly, waving good-bye. In the background, the crickets were serenading continuously. The brooks streamed with their currents of water, sliding through the rocks. Idyllic waterfalls with rainbows cascaded along their own natural path.

At last, the group arrived at their destination to a beautiful house with a surrounding garden, where they were greeted by a middle aged man in casual dress. Jimki went out running to see a playful kitten on the moist grass dampened by the foggy and misty air. The tallness of the green pine trees in the background made the house resemble a cottage in a forest. During the British colonial period, the wooden house served as a summer residence of a British high court judge. Bithi was interested in taking a tour around the living quarters.

The wooden floors inside were accented with decorative Indian rugs. A spiral staircase led up to bedrooms that housed an elegant decor that had a bit of English country cottage style. The windows were accented with glass and wood shutters. From the window, Bithi saw the dwellings of the local people a bit higher up. Then there were green pine trees again and, in a slightly higher elevation, rows of the same kind of dwellings. Still farther away, she saw the snow-capped mountain. Bithi could not believe she was looking at the majestic peaks of Kachanjungha.

The houses were in a state of disrepair with discolored wooden staircases likely to break. The landscape and the sights of local people's dwellings made her feel that the gorgeous landscape was outlined by an ancient discolored frame. She felt sad at the sight of the dwellings of local residents. *Someone should do something to improve their situation,* she thought. *I should ask my mother.*

Renuka called her daughters, "We are going to have our dinner early. We have to get up early in the morning. We will get ready by three a.m.," she said, "We are going to Tiger Hill to watch the sunrise."

The next morning the group bundled up and took a few extra blankets as well. The station wagon started honking bright and early, and the group boarded the wagon driven by a man named Tej Bahadur. The station wagon started climbing the winding path; it was dark and chilly. Sometimes the ascent was slow, but most of the time it sped along steadily. The path was so narrow that it felt like one wheel was almost outside the road. The darkness was moving retrograde like a continuous black sheet as they pushed forward.

Mr. Bahadur brought the group to their destination at the famous Tiger Hill. He was familiar with the area so he pointed out a place from where we could see it best. There were other people besides this group, all eager and ready to see the sunrise. Renuka's group got closer and put blankets around themselves as it was very chilly.

Darkness of the fading evening slowly morphed into the light of early morning; there was a glow on the horizon. Suddenly the clouds and the fog started imbuing an orange tinge. The fog and the clouds were passing very close; the girls could feel the damp cool touch of it over one's face.

The rays of light from the eastern horizon glided along the peaks of Kanchanjungha. It traveled through the mist and pierced the pine forest and came around. Bithi and Jimki were excited to touch it and realized that one could not do that, just enjoy and feel the sensation of joy and wonder in their heart.

The rays of the sun started playing their victorious overture. Everyone was under a spell. It seemed like an eternity, where time was not moving. Bithi did not want it to move, it was so beautiful. People cried out loud, "The green! The violet! The orange! The blue and red!" The sun slowly and gloriously rose beyond Kanchanjungha. The magnificent snow-capped peak gradually changed from orange to red.

The overture of colors played and surrounded them; they were enveloped by a river of floating colors. Some people were singing to the glory of nature from a famous Tagore poem. Some were chanting Sanskrit hymns to the sun and offering prayers. The mountains echoed their songs to the glory of the sun. The birds started chirping, while the pine forest was murmuring a heartfelt song to the glory of nature.

In the meantime, sunlight sprinkled the golden color to the peaks of Kachanjungha. It started dazzling like real gold. Everyone was speechless and awestruck. Peace and tranquility heightened their senses. Bithi gazed at this sensational sunrise. She stood motionless, completely lost in her imagination in an unknown land, floating in the timeless depths of eternity.

A Tale Before Halloween

The evening was filled with the anticipation of rain, with the cool breeze whispering through the leaves of the live oak trees. It was just before Halloween.

I was finishing up hanging my yearly decorations as my next-door neighbor Chris noticed me.

"I love your year-round enthusiasm about the festivity," she quipped. "Do people celebrate Halloween in India?"

I smiled. "No, not really, but we have a day in Bengal before Diwali known as *The Bhut Chaturdashi*," I replied. "It is almost the same time of year as Halloween."

Chris inquired further about the holiday, so I felt honored to share the custom even though I knew it would be a challenge.

"Those not from India may find the holiday difficult to grasp but I will try to do my best to explain it." I motioned for Chris to take a seat on the front porch bench as I sat across from her. She waited for me to begin.

"*Bhut*," I explained, "means ghost, but literally it means 'the past.' *Chaturdashi* is the 14th day of the new moon phase; that is to say that the 15th day is the new moon."

"We put fourteen candles at different corners of the house and prepare a special kind of dish with fourteen different greens along with other dishes. Then we sit around and chat with our families, talk about scary things and share ghost stories."

"That's such an interesting custom to share and I'm eager to know more," Chris replied.

I found myself spinning a tale woven by memories of past events from my childhood. I told Chris about the things that were scary to me, such as creepy creatures like snakes, centipedes and spiders, and imaginary things like ghosts and spirits. When we were young, my best friend Amita and I talked about these creepy mysterious snake-like creatures. They were always in our mythological stories, such as the one about Vishnu, the supreme energy, who lay dreaming of the Universe on a bed made of the body of a big fat live snake named Adishesa. Amita and I discussed how it would feel to lie down on a bed made of the body of a big fat live snake. We felt like vomiting as we imagined the slimy body with scales.

"These are real creatures and if by mistake you step on them, they will bite and you will die within a short period if you are not attended to properly," I told Chris.

"Have you seen a live snake running or crawling?" Chris asked me.

I nodded. "I saw a snake running around a field like a wave beyond the bungalow of my Grandfather's vacation home where we went for a short visit. It was the King Cobra, whose body is silvery gray with some black dots spread over its long body." I shuddered. "When it was slithering it looked like a silver colored stream of gracefully gliding water. These creatures can stand and fan their heads and if you're in their way, they bite you and you are banished to the other world."

Chris gasped. "What happens to people who go there?"

I shook my head. "That I do not know. The tribal people beat the snake to death as they thought that this snake was surely going to attack someone. They dragged the long body of the dead snake and cut its head off to take out the poison from the fangs. The rest of the body was used for cooking and eating."

Chris shivered. "That's disgusting."

My own body filled with goosebumps remembering the event.

I thought about another story I knew about a good snake, one who fanned its head like an umbrella and protected a Prince from a storm in a forest. This forest was cursed and the storm would start if anybody ventured there—it was a forest the Prince was destined to travel through as he was seeking a cave on the mountain, which held a treasure his Grandparents had left him.

Amid the sudden storm, the Prince, the snake gave the Prince a bright jewel from its head, assuring the Prince's safekeeping. Knowing the jewel had the power to protect the Prince from evil when he needed it, the snake disappeared.

Chris was very pleased to hear these stories but had to say good-bye to take care of things at her home. I finished putting up the rest of the decorations, very pleased with what I surveyed in front of me: pumpkins with faces, a dangling skeleton on my front door, the spider webs and spiders all over my potted plants. Satisfied that the whole effect was spooky enough, I went back inside.

I looked at the clock—it was almost bedtime.

❧❧❧

As the flashes of the story continually forged their way to me, I became overpowered by a magical moment. My heavy eyes began to focus on everything around me moving far away and with an unknown force. Suddenly, I was ten years old. I was pushed forward toward a place that was beyond my control and I continued to travel until I stopped in front of a mysterious Being dressed in a silver outfit. The Being looked like an astronaut and somehow I assumed it was the Prince in the story in his quest for the unknown.

As I looked at him, he made note of my presence, but didn't immediately engage me. I found myself very close to him, almost attached to him. He finally turned to me and said, "Let's go, you are my shadow."

My eyebrows furrowed as I pondered the concept. *I was his shadow? How was that possible?*

"That is interesting," I replied, my thoughts still circulating, trying to digest the reality, or in this case, the "surreality" of this encounter as our journey began.

I watched as this Being—which I couldn't quite discern was human or something altogether different—put on a headgear with winged protrusions on either side and place two thick gold anklets on his ankles. He motioned for me to follow. He hovered briefly above the ground and then off we went.

I noticed how the green fields and houses were moving further down, while we moved upwards. The birds flew over us to inspect what kind of creatures we were as the cold breeze pierced through us and we moved further up through the clouds. I didn't feel any movement. It felt like we were suspended in the clouds, which were like fluffy cotton balls below.

"Shadow, are you all right?" the Being asked.

"I am not a shadow," I replied. "I am a ten-year-old girl."

He laughed. "Okay, then you are a shadowy little girl."

I asked him where he was going and what his mission was and he did not provide a specific answer. "You will find out soon enough," he said. I was dazed, willing myself to open my eyes fully, but could not. After a while I felt we were descending in a spiral fashion.

Down below, the entire vast green area was gradually coming into view as my eyes focused on green fields, a river, hills and mountains with meadows. There were beautiful tall green trees and flowering shrubs growing all over. The houses in this landscape looked like Toyland during the holidays.

Since I didn't know the name of the Being who insisted on accompanying me, I decided to call him Man Without a Name—MWN, for short. For some reason I felt he was a male.

MWN addressed me with the title that I had yet to become accustomed. "Shadow," he said, "the people in this region are very happy and peaceful and they help each other. They make their own rules and regulations and strictly follow them. They select someone to be the leader who has to follow the rules made by the people. This particular place or world is called Sujhan."

I shook my head. Nothing was making sense. What kind of leader had to follow rules made by the people? Whatever happened to "Follow the Leader?" I longed to crack that joke to MWN but I doubted he'd get it.

"Do they have day and night and seasons like we have on Earth?" I asked.

"Yes they do, but they are bathed by a different sun and moon in a different planetary system," MWN replied. My head failed to come up with an explanation about how I came to another planetary system. In the meantime, we landed in a place where there were aircraft that looked like decorated sledges.

৯৯৯

MWN was greeted and accompanied by several persons dressed with long colorful satin outfits decorated with sequins and jewels. The beautiful women wore their long black hair in a bun with fresh flowers around it. Their colorful dresses had pleated flowing skirts and their tops were adorned with either flowing scarves around their shoulders or a decorated veil on their heads. Each woman was adorned with different jewelry and dangling gold earrings, studded with precious stones in different sizes. They looked like the cave paintings from Ajanta that I once saw in a picture book at our house.

Still confused about my role as a "shadow," I followed MWN, who proved to be an able guide, to a big mansion that appeared to belong to some renowned and important person.

I had no doubt that I would be there with him.

We were led by a group of people dressed colorfully in satin as we passed through different arch-like structures that showcased chandeliers of various sizes and shapes. The mosaic floors were emblazoned with multicolor stone chips. We came to a big chamber where on either side there were decorated pillars. In the middle of the chamber were strips of embroidered silken rug-like material running from the entrance of the chamber to a broad big sofa-like structure where a man was sitting. I considered him to be good looking and approachable when he greeted us with a smile and showed an eagerness to listen to MWN. Then he called a few other people, pointing to a map and directing MWN how to proceed. The man, who appeared to be the leader, said that he would help us travel to the end of his and his people's world.

"At the edge," the Leader said, "there is a big mountain where you will enter through a cave. You will find a tunnel that is powered with an invisible force that will draw you downward. When you reach the bottom there will be an opening and then you will feel a sudden state of emptiness. You have to proceed with confidence through this nothingness," said the Leader.

There was a moment of silence as I caught myself holding my breath.

"If you fail you are doomed, no one will ever find you," the Leader said, his eyes directed to me. "Beyond that is another world—the world of Not Human."

I pondered what the Leader said. He continued. "The inhabitants of this world are human, but different. They look like humans from the outside but they are cruel and hard as a stone. They have no feelings." I shuddered as the Leader continued. He warned that the Not Human had evolved to be always suspicious, antagonistic, jealous, and selfish. Sometimes they showed that they were nice. This was but a dangerous tactic of theirs.

"These creatures lure you, then they trap and squeeze you mentally and physically until you suffer the torture they enjoy administering," the Leader said. "No one from other worlds dare to enter their world."

"I have a mission," MWN spoke up. "As a messenger of time, I know that events must keep on rolling. Your honor, I would like to remind you that time is a pivotal thing that bring changes in the Universe. It is like a flowing river—it has to flow; so if there is a block or hurdle the flow will not go on. Time randomly selects parts of its flowing body to create messengers and shapes like us and sends them to different parts of the Universe," MWN continued. "After we finish our work we go and unite with time itself, the flowing entity, and are happy. That, to us, is our home."

I stood listening as MWN continued to explain.

"Time in the world of Not Human, where one of our messengers is trapped, is not moving smoothly. The people there are stagnant and cold, moving round and round with their vices," he said.

The Leader then spoke. "The people have to realize what they are doing is not right and then the change will come. I wish you all the best for your efforts to release your trapped fellow messenger. We honor all creatures: lions, tigers, foxes, elephants, snakes, and birds. We all live in peaceful coexistence and all creatures are given the utmost respect by us. You are welcome to pass again through our world—if you survive your quest."

At this point I realized what a big mission I had been thrown in the middle of and began to ask myself, *Why I am here?*

"Shadow, I need you, that's why you are here," MWN suddenly said to me, reading my thoughts.

Still surprised that he knew what I was thinking, I replied, "If I am just a shadow, as you say, there is nothing useful about me. I am a shadow with one dimension." As far as I knew, shadows in my world, at least, served but one purpose: to follow. *A shadow, I reasoned, wasn't a born leader.*

MWN glared at me. "Stop talking like that. You are surely multi-dimensional. Otherwise, you wouldn't be here."

Our journey to the unknown continued. Whatever the Leader of Sujhan mentioned we encountered—despite the dark cave, faint lights could be seen in the distance, showing us our way. The source of the lights that guided us came from jewels on snakes' heads, yet I didn't fear the snakes and only saw the light.

Oh, what a ride we took in the dark tunnel as we were pushed and pulled and squeezed like rubber bands. I was attached to MWN and was more lightweight so this push and pull force was not so much on me. I remembered how my father once told me that there were holes or tunnels in which time could become lost. *Oh no, what will happen if MWN, the messenger of time, gets lost?* I shuddered.

In time, we reached the bottom and suddenly I heard a shriek. MWN managed to get himself out. Then there was the nothingness. Suddenly I was in front of MWN. He started screaming, "Do not go in front! Follow me!"

I was confused, silently begging him to stop screaming. *I have no control,'* I thought. *I really am a shadow.*

We stepped into the nothingness, but it seemed to be a spongy, dark, gooey entity. We paddled hard on the mossy substance and with a lot of effort kept ourselves afloat until we came upon a shore. At last we reached the land of Not Human. "Why I am here what's my role?"

MWN replied, "I will let you know soon." I sighed but couldn't detect the expression on the Being's stoic face.

"I will change myself to mere particles," MWN told me.

He must've seen the shocked look on my face. "What and how do you do that? What will be my existence?"

MWN now seemed very eager to answer my question as he raised his hand, signaling the importance of what he was about to say. "You will also be a phantom of shadowy particles. I have said what I can about this matter for it is far beyond your comprehension. Now that you've seen the place, you can say this is another world!" he proclaimed.

I saw what lay before me: trees, grass, mountains and valleys brimming with green as far as the eye could see. They looked very much like the world I came from, only they seemed to shimmer with strange light.

"We have to ascend the mountain," MWN informed me. As we proceeded, I observed MWN become a cluster of particles and I become phantom particles, just as MWN had said. We moved forward up the mountain and reaching a big castle. The fierce armed guards there were monitoring the area in front of automatic iron gates.

The guards could not see us, as we were a cluster of particles; but their monitors showed some background noise—they could not figure out the source of it. We hovered around briefly and then went in.

The people there were very serious, with expressions of anxiety and fear on their faces. Some gritted their teeth, others tightened their jaws and took short breaths. We pushed forward. We came across two people arguing, both antagonistic. All of a sudden an armed guard came and started kicking them.

Yes, I am a cluster of phantom particles, I thought, *but I still have my sense of vision.*

As MWN's instructed me, my work was to become a real shadow again, but this time I had to attach myself to a prison guard in a particular dungeon where the other messenger of time was imprisoned.

While I was crafting my plan of action, we found the dungeon just in time to see a female messenger of time in shackles. She was imprisoned in a dungeon made of a thick material, which had a continuous gravitational pull that sucked the messenger of time towards the floor. There was no escape for her. She was suspended there in an altered state of consciousness. The door was operated by a switchbox on the wall outside the dungeon that had an iron lid. Somehow I knew that the key to the lid was with the guard.

The monitor close to the dungeon was continuously signaling the state of affairs inside the dungeon as we hovered around the guard and got our bearings. We both realized how difficult the task before us was.

This particular imprisoned messenger came to the world of Not Human to let the inhabitants know that they could live very happily if they tried to change their outlook of living. She implored them not to burden themselves with things that would not move time smoothly or else they would go round and round in a stagnant pool of time without any happiness and progress for the future. The ruler of the Not Human World did not understand this and felt threatened and imprisoned the messenger.

The task before us now was to free the messenger. MWN hovered over the head of the guard while I attached myself to the guard as a shadow. The guard was startled at first and performed different maneuvers to try to get my shadow off. By maneuvering him, I tried to pull him towards the wall where the key was hidden.

He obeyed and retrieved the key and went to check the messenger of time and flipped the switch to open the door. As the messenger came floating up, I gyrated in a dance-like move. The confused guard danced along with me as he was forced to repeat my movements.

The MWN pulled the messenger by signaling her as a cluster of particles. The messenger of time returned to consciousness and soon they were both up in the air out of the dungeon. I detached myself from the guard and while he was disoriented, I traveled up in the sky with MWN and with the other messenger of time.

In the meantime, the world of Not Human was on high alert. Beepers and sirens screeched and we could see they were after us, shooting laser-like beams in our direction. Our pursuers were not sure where myself and MWN were, but they could see the other messenger of time. We did our best to disguise her and escaped by sinking inside a dark mass—a good hiding place for the time being. For the moment, we were out of sight. After a time we continued, reaching the dark gooey material of nothingness. We swam across the big ocean of darkness and with a lot of effort and hard work we came to a lighted shore, where we could walk normally.

This was far from the end of our journey as we had to enter yet another tunnel, enduring the push and pull force that caused the messenger, like us, to act as though we were string-like creatures that at the end came out shrieking. I worried that we would get lost in the tunnel forever.

"I know what you're thinking, Shadow," MWN told me. "These tunnels are not the giant ones that swallow everything inside them, even entire entities like us."

"Kind of like time," I murmured.

"Yes, you have good knowledge and under-standing," MWN said, continuing his comment that among the vast Universe holes like this existed where you could travel through to other locations.

MWN expressed how grateful he was for how skillfully I kept the guard busy with my dance poses so that the other messenger could escape from the prison. The other messenger nodded requesting that she be called "Kalam" which means 'time' in Sanskrit. Smiling to myself, it felt strange in this unknown world recognizing such a familiar word.

"We are again approaching the world of Sujhan," MWN announced solemnly. One question that had haunted me since I met MWN urgently had to be asked: "How could time be an entity and if it is, is there a beginning and an end?"

MWN seemed surprised by my question.

"Shadow, you ask a very challenging question— one which has an esoteric answer—but I'll try to simplify it." Scratching his chin, he looked beyond the horizon and said, "There is indeed a beginning and there is an end. It is hard to understand all the laws of creation as they are going round and round in their own circle's bend. So the understanding of beginning and end is difficult. But do not worry—the end is not going to be soon and if the continuum we are in ends, there will be another continuum to follow and another dimensional time. All these are bounded by a universal law, which dictates the universe in every way. It ultimately binds each and everything that exists in the universe so far as we are conscious about it."

I felt very relieved and entering the world of Sujhan, we could see the familiar valleys and meadows, the mountains and trees with just the right touch of changing colors. The houses below again looked like children's toys.

We saw some sledge-like aircraft coming close to us. What fun they must have had making a welcome sign for us! Within time, we were directed to descend to a designated area, a mountainous region that looked like a naturally built open-air auditorium. We paused there as the Leader of Sujhan greeted us, accompanied by his aides holding flowers and banners.

Although I was still a shadow, everyone acknow-ledged my presence.

There was an announcement that a show was about to start. This was the last show before the year ending, because all the animals and creatures that lived on the mountain would be hibernating soon.

Kicking off the show was a parade of elephants, which made their way around a ring along with adorable baby elephants pulling up their curled up snouts. Beautiful tigers lined up in a row roaring powerfully together as male lions shook their manes and joined in the roaring and the females followed with their young ones. Giraffes with their proud long necks strode casually as the zebras hastily trotted away. Oh, what a sight to behold as massive gorillas beat their chests. By this time, it was already getting dark. The sky was studded with stars as the moon peeped through a patch of clouds. The fireflies commenced their dance and crickets serenaded the crowd. A pack of wolves howled up at the luminous moon. Then the slithery cobras came and started dancing, the jewels on their heads illuminating the area as they swayed their heads side to side and coiled their bodies up. A huge white owl hooted triumphantly as the snakes bowed their heads and left one by one. The hyena's laughter broke the monotony of the crickets' serenade, as the gray owls hooted from the branches of trees declaring the night's end. As the night was slowly dying down, a faint light cast on the eastern horizon just as the nightingales sang their last song before soaring up in the sky. *What a night*, I thought, and as I stretched my legs, I kicked something and found myself back in my bed, my feet touching a wooden board at the foot of my bed. I heard my pet bird chirping away, obviously repeating words he had learned from me.

"I love you. Pretty, pretty birdie."

I looked outside as the sun set on the horizon and the rays of sun pierced through the fog and made its way to our yard. In a daze, I kept on looking at the misty landscape, not wanting to wake up from my dreamy world or to forget this marvelous adventure.

Silhouettes of Time

I.
The Way to Noaykhali

❧

As the black clouds started gathering, big drops of rain came down making chattering sounds that filled the air. The dry and dusty ground started quenching its thirst as the scent of fresh earth filled the air. The year 1946 would prove to be unforgettable for a young man about to begin his journey to an unknown fate that was his and his alone, for no other man was destined for as much greatness as Arun.

❧❧❧

The big city of Calcutta located on the east bank of the Hooghly River in 1946 was shaking with the unrest of communal riot between the Hindus and Muslims, just before the Independence of India. Trains loaded with refugees coming from east Bengal were trying to reach a safe haven. Sick, hungry fear-stricken men, women and children huddled together came to take refuge in Calcutta. Those murdered by attackers laid in some of the compartments. Their dead bodies and putrefied smell magnified the landscape of horror in the situation.

ﬞ❧❧❧

Arun tried to remember the pleasant train ride when he would visit his mother at their home in Majer Gathi, a small town in the east part of Bengal.

He would sit very close to the window and survey the green landscape passing by as mile after mile of green paddy fields swayed amid the gentle breeze, moving backwards as the train moved forward. Verdant green pastures as far as the eye could see blanketed the fields as the infinite dome of blue sky formed a canopy over the green landscape. Two tall palm trees were swaying, their leaves murmuring as a young girl with a red-bordered yellow sari carrying a basket ran across the paddy fields where men and women were busy working. The reflection on the window mirror of the train with passengers moving side to side in the compartment with the motion of the train and the reflection of the passing green landscape created a feeling of surreal beauty. Arun's heart filled with tranquility and joy.

❧❧❧

His mother lived with one of his elder brothers in a place called Ballygunge in the south part of the vast Calcutta cityscape.

Even as Arun clinched his jaw and gritted his teeth when thunder rumbled and lightning flashed, matching his mood, he didn't want to agonize over the fact that his mother fled their home in Majergathi as the riot between Hindus and Muslim broke in India.

∽ঔ∽ঔ∽ঔ

When he was a young man, Arun was imprisoned twice since 1940 and was released for few months but was back again a few months later.

Being one of the revolutionaries fighting against British rule in India made Arun a frequent prisoner and enemy of the oppressors. Arun could not fathom the communal riot between the Hindus and Muslims. His restlessness and anxiety grew more and more like a storm twister as he agonized over how their ancestral home in Majer Gathi in district Khulna in East Bengal was destroyed as a result of the strife.

His mother had escaped through their backyard garden in the dark and sunk herself in their lovely pond so she wouldn't be detected by the perpetrators. When the coast was clear, she walked through the ditches of the muddy rice fields all night until she caught a bus to a train station.

He remembered how when his uncle was murdered, his blood spilled all over the courtyard where they used to play. His cousins had fled town on a vegetable truck, hiding behind piles of vegetables, seeking refuge at a Red Cross center and then escaped and had not been heard from since.

Arun clinched his teeth and punched the pillow in anger at the banishment of his family. He got up paced all night, determined to do something to restore peace in his homeland but he knew that he was just one man trying to take on a mighty foe.

He decided to disguise himself as a Muslim cleric because if he rode the train to East Bengal as a Hindu, he would be murdered.

The thought of leaving Calcutta without telling his mother and agonizing over how he planned to tell Sikhrini, the love of his life, began to weigh heavily on Arun as he sat on the edge of bed and looked around the room. He went to his desk, got hold of a writing pad and started scribbling for few minutes, then he threw his writing pad and started walking to the door, murmuring, "I will get a taxi."

As he walked for a while through an avenue of street lights, Arun felt these inanimate objects trying to tell him something and he found himself looking for some kind of sign. The stars struggled to break through a screen of artificial light amid the dark sky to look down at him.

Tonight, restless Calcutta was drowsy as only a few taxis zoomed by.

"It is not wise to see my mother," he muttered to himself. "I cannot leave seeing her anxious face, it will be too painful."

Arun wondered about how his love, Sikhrini and what she might be doing at this late hour. He still faced a dilemma about whether he should write a letter to both of them. Finally, he decided to write a quick note before leaving.

To his mother he apologized for putting her through this much anxiety.

To Sikhrini, he wrote:

I bid you farewell for now, my love, but not forever for I am going to pursue a mission to establish a Peace Camp in East Bengal. I do not know how, but I am sure with my strong willpower I can do it. And while it pains me to say this my love, I say if you find somebody you wish to be with or if your parents arrange for you to settle, you have my reluctant blessing for I wish you every happiness even if it may bring me so much pain. If you can, please visit my mother, as she loves you so as if you were her very own daughter. I know I will have the strength to carry out my task that comes only out of your love. So I hope to survive this task and come back to you if you are still willing to wait for me. I will be all yours now and forever, Arun.

The train from Sealdah station of Calcutta started its journey with Arun on board, riding along still mired in dilemma in the dark toward the unknown.

Disguised as a Muslim cleric with a white cap and long beard, Arun's appearance managed to appear convincing enough to onlookers as he sat on a corner seat and scanned the compartment where the dim light inside the compartment helped his disguise. Illuminated only by a tiny light which cast hues of gray, Arun could barely make out the sight of a corpse lying at the far end of the compartment. The dead body covered with blood was that of a male whose hollow open eyes faced the ceiling.

Sharing a compartment with a dead body made Arun feel as though a python had squeezed the life out of him. He was unable to sleep that night.

To his relief, he arrived at his destination to witness people at the train station wanting to cross the border with their luggage in tow, running through a temporary barricade. Since Arun had no belongings, it was easy for him to join the stream of people on the other side.

He still had to travel by a bus and then take a ferry to reach his final destination. It was early morning in Noaykhali, where at the break of dawn, a red glow in the eastern sky caressed the earth's surface. Suddenly Arun's eyes caught a charred paddy field in the distance. The landscape was nearly all black with some patches of smoldering fire that continued a slow and steady burn. His eyes then cast upon a small green patch of paddy field hopelessly trying to hold itself up amid the acrid smell of smoke that filled the air.

After an uneventful bus ride, Arun, still disguised as a Muslim cleric, came to Ferry Ghat, where he took a small boat instead of a large one. The boat man helpfully guided Arun on how to go to the places where he would face the least confrontation. The boatman said there were areas where the Hindus were fighting back, but assured him that ultimately the Hindus would lose.

Arun was grateful for that information and wanted to go to the area where people were trying hard to fight back and defend themselves. So he got down around the boundary of Noaykhali.

"Noaykhali is in the southeastern part of east Bengal located in the district of Chittagong," said a man who gave Arun directions. "This area is bordered by the Comilla district and lies to the north of the Megna River estuary and the Bay of Bengal to the south."

Arun listened as the guide told him more about the region. The ancient name of Noaykhali was Bhulua. It was seriously affected by flood water of the Dhakatia river from Trpura hills. To salvage the situation, a canal was dug from Dakatia to Ramganj Place, Sanaimuri and Chaumahani to divert the water flow to the junction of the river Megna and Feni. After excavating the long canal "Bhulua" began known as Noaykhali. The name Noaykhali originated from the terms *Noa* (New) and *Khal* (Canal). The district represented an extensive flat coastal and delta land, located on the tidal plain of the Megna

River delta. Around Noaykhali on three sides was an alluvial plain annually inundated and fertilized by slit deposition from Megna estuary.

The place was very fertile for agriculture and people lived happily and peacefully, taking advantage of the resources around them until the communal riot broke between Hindus and Muslims.

Arun walked towards the area where the Hindus were living with fear of being attacked. On his way Arun saw some burnt houses as a breeze seeped through the deserted and damaged homes that began making a crackling sound from the pain of being burned.

As he came across a combination scorched and verdant green paddy fields, Arun sought refuge behind a tree where he changed from the Muslim cleric outfit to his regular attire and continued to move on. Sometime later, he found the village where he was supposed to meet Dhiren, a brave man he had heard was trying to defend other fellow Hindus.

Tired, thirsty and hungry, Arun arrived at an open courtyard, where he saw some people were engaged in a serious discussion. He could tell that his sudden appearance startled the group, who gasped in surprise.

Arun made an attempt to show them he wasn't a threat by warmly introducing himself.

"I came all the way from Calcutta. I would like to meet Dhiren, if he is available, and I am here to help you," Arun said.

Their expression instantly changed from suspicion to very courteous as they invited him to sit with them and a woman appeared and handed him a cup of chai. As Arun listened, his eyes scanned the courtyard. There was a moderate sized, neatly kept hut in front where the group, who figured he was tired from his journey, directed him as a place for him to stay, if he wished. They spread a mat made of palm leaves in the front verandah of the hut. A lady came out from inside and offered him coconut water to drink.

It was quite a treat for Arun after the long journey. One of the group members, Prafulla, came forward and said, "I am going to Dhiren's house and inform him that you are here and wish to meet him."

Arun thanked Prafulla who mentioned that it wouldn't take long to get to Dhiren. "Please wait and rest here." While Arun was enjoying his drink, the rest of the group arrived at the hut and introduced themselves. Shankar addressed him as "Dada," meaning elder brother: "What is your plan and how will you help us, Dada? With all due respect, how will we know that you are trustworthy?"

Arun anticipated these types of questions. "Well," he said, "we all have to plan and actively work together in the process of helping each other. I have to know what sort of immediate difficulties you are facing now."

In the midst of their discussion, Prafulla returned with the man Arun traveled so far to see. Dhiren was tall and well built, with muscular arms, and his dark brown skin glistened with a healthy shine from sweat. His face was somewhat round with big black eyes sparkling like fresh morning light. He had a sharp nose in a well-shaven face and a butterfly mustache, with its two pointed ends turned up.

He nodded to Arun, and with his palms together, greeted him with, "*Namaskar.*"

Arun replied: "*Namaskar.* I am here to help you. First of all, we have to plan how we will proceed, but I want to continue to discuss the problems needing immediate attention."

"We Hindus are in a helpless position," Dhiren said. "We are in danger as an attacker may come at any time to burn our rice granary, attack our women and children, kill the males of the family, destroy and burn our living quarters."

Dhiren said that they had tried to send signs that the members of the camp are more than prepared to defend themselves, but their messages to their oppressors fell on deaf ears.

"They threatened us that they would come back with more men and get us out from here," he told Arun. "The police are not cooperating with us." Dhiren looked at the group, some of them nodding their heads. "They have actually been helping the attackers, burning our rice fields and the rice granary so that we all will die of hunger."

Dhiren continued his diatribe in lightning speed, then looked at Arun for a possible solution.

Arun took a deep breath. "First of all, I need some land, about an acre or two, to build some houses or huts like this, that will have a fence. I need a place there to stay and organize our camp and we will all take turns and do our best to run the place and train to defend ourselves. The place we build will provide shelter to women and children who have lost their loved ones and need protection. We will slowly start to prepare food for the needy people. There will be doctors on duty to treat the sick people and ultimately recruit some nursing staff. We will name the place, 'Peace Camp.' But most important, right now, we need to prepare to defend ourselves from the attackers."

Everyone in unison bellowed: "Yes!"

"We can build the small huts, as many as you like, and fence them in no time. Two acres of land or more we can get. But how do we defend ourselves?" Shankar asked.

Arun began to pace as he folded his arms, a determined expression on his face. "We have to learn the tactics of ancient armory and martial arts of India. Dhiren, I know you are an expert in Indian *Talawar* (sword) fight."

Dhiren nodded as Arun continued. "You should start training others also. Is anyone here an expert in *Latti* fight?" Arun was referring to a defense tactic that involved the use of tall rounded bamboo trunks included in the ancient armory of India.

A broad-shouldered, muscular man named Suren came forward. "Yes!"

Arun nodded. "You should start to train the others in that defense tactic as well so we can form a group of fighters who can defend themselves and others. You should also try to train the women, too." Arun paused to scan the group of women assembled.

Nagen, another local resident, addressed Arun with the local title of respect.

"Dada, the attackers come with open fire torches and start shouting *Allah ho Akbar* from a distance then are soon joined by others from different villages in the dark. They then come racing with vengeance and destroy everything we have. It is nerve wracking to hear that sound in the dead of night," Nagen said, as the others in the group nodded their heads woefully.

Arun nodded again in understanding. "I am aware that circumstances are frightful. And so we must learn to control our fear and concentrate on how we can best proceed with our plan."

Arun then proceeded to direct various people to do certain tasks while still addressing the group as a whole.

"Please get some oxen, at least fifty male Mahish, bison-like animals which we will keep handy," he said. They will be first ones to charge the attackers by forming a stampede and then, those armed with swords will be all set to charge, followed by those trained in the *Latti* tactics.

"The women who wish to join us in this fight will serve as a backup regiment that I shall personally support and help lead in this fight," he addressed to the brave women in the crowd who had gathered.

Arun told them their slogans would be: *"Hare Murare Madhu Kautaba Bhare* and *Bande mataram.* "The first one is a Sanskrit hymn or *Sloka* taking the name of Vishnu and Krishna who destroyed the evil monster-like creature and the second one is 'Glory to our Mother,' " Arun said. "We will all shout our slogans, even those who are not confronting the attackers. Please secretly spread the news that when, in the dead of night, they hear sounds of slogans, whether they hear it properly or not, to ask them to chant *Hare Murare Madhu Kaitabha Bhare.* The sounds will be like echoes and will weaken the morale of the attacker, thinking for the time being that people are coming from different directions to fight them. Please remember we are not going to confront them unless they come and attack us; the whole plan is for our defense. We have to rebuild, defend and regain our confidence to fight this ordeal. Are you all with me?"

The crowd gathered stood up and roared a resounding, "Yes!"

Arun placed his palms together and closed his eyes as the people continued their cheers of support.

One of the men stood up to speak on behalf of the group. "Yes, we are with you and plan to start building the Peace Camp immediately."

Arun asked for suggestions on where the camp might be placed. Amal raised his hand and said, "I know exactly where. I have some open space I am going to donate, the entire two acres for the Peace Camp."

So they all cheered and promised to start building their Peace Camp the first thing the next morning.

Dhiren came forward and invited Arun to stay with him in his house as long as he wished as well as to dine with him and his family.

Peace Camp building began bright and early the next morning as promised. During the course of building the camp and the training of the makeshift army in the martial arts and self defense tactics, the enemy twice attempted a sneak attack, only to be thwarted by the new-found skills of the defenders.

As planned, the bulls and the Mahish, bison-like animal, were the first line of action along with torches of open fire set free. Frantic, the animals charged the attackers, stampeding them recklessly.

Behind them, the people held firm shiny *talwar* (swords) as they marched forward, chanting slogans: *Hare Mure* and *Bande mataram.* The chanting helped the morale of all the Hindus. The chanting in the dark, which came from other surrounding villages created some kind of mysterious and eerie feeling, which weakened the morale of the attackers.

The dream project of a Peace Camp was so well established that Mahatma Gandhi himself came and stayed in the camp, further boosting the morale of the people. The Peace Camp provided a safe haven to the children, whose parents were murdered. Displaced people were suitably placed in homes in and around Calcutta.

For orphan girls and boys special boarding schools were established around the outskirts of Calcutta to provide them with proper education and skills for their future.

Mahatma Gandhi took personal interest in the success of the Peace Camp and the other nationalist leaders came to survey the situation and endeavored to help the distressed people.

Before the Peace Camp's security was fortified and the members trained in defense tactics, a large number of young girls were abducted by the attackers. Now, even attempted abductions were thwarted with most of the girls rescued from their abductors and placed in secure refuges close to their family. Some were sent to residential schools surrounded by trained armed forces. Great care was taken to secure each child in a placement where they were looked after by Peace Camp defenders who would check on them periodically to ensure each place was suitable for the girl or the boy in their respective habitats.

But alas, despite its success, the Peace Camp had to be closed abruptly as India was divided. People who were living and working in the Peace Camp had to leave Noaykhali and move to the Indian side of Bengal. Arun tried his best to place people in and around Calcutta.

Ultimately, Arun himself had to leave. So on the last day, he went around the deserted Peace Camp saying goodbye, remembering the first time he landed here months ago, armed with anxiety but lots of determination to help the distressed people. Even as he stood there, he wondered if he did in fact succeed in doing that.

His soul searching continued as he came to Ferry Ghat, a kind of port. This time he took a larger boat along with several people going to the Indian side of Bengal. From there, he boarded a train to Calcutta.

On the train he took a window seat just as the train started to chug along. As the green landscape on this side of Bengal started fading away in the background, Arun looked sadly outside. He could not believe that part of Bengal was going to be lost for so many people—a region which was once their home sweet home.

As the train started to accelerate, Arun felt the landscapes pass by like patches of green lost forever in the past. He imagined the map of India and was startled, thinking it looked like somebody had chopped parts of the body of Mother India. He sighed, shaking his head.

The train's speed coasted along at a normal rate to match his beating heart.

Arun felt a lightness he hadn't felt in a long time. He was finally going back to see his mother who would be very pleased. He could nearly picture the smile on her face.

Outside in the passing landscape, Arun spotted a couple sitting under a shade of a Banyan tree and then it happened.

Sikhrini's face flashed in his mind as his heart started beating faster.

II.
Taxi Driver to Judge

❧

Arun watched, mesmerized, as the ceiling fan circulated making a whining high-pitched sound as if it excitedly wanted to tell a story. The room was in a court house, a chamber where the judges come and relax during their recess.

In front of Arun lay stacks of court case files. The smell of an old court house, with its deep scent of antique mahogany seemed to linger from when the British ruled India. Arun, in 1962, fifteen years since India's independence, was even more contemplative. The court house remained unchanged since British rule in India, with the exception of seeing faces of all local Indian citizens working in the court house.

The attendant with a red turban and white buttoned-up coat knocked at the door. "Sir, here is your tea."

"Come in," Arun replied.

"And here is the newspaper, Sir."

Surprised, Arun asked, "Why do you show me the newspaper?"

The attendant blinked his eyes. "Sir, this is the local paper, the *Amrita Bazar Patrika*. There is a full page of story on you."

"There is?" Arun had no recollection of being interviewed for a newspaper article recently.

"Sir, you can see for yourself," the attendant said and placed the newspaper on the desk. "And a taxi driver from the Taxi Drivers Association is here to see you."

Arun was growing impatient with these unexpected events. "You know better that I am not supposed to see anyone when court is in session."

But the attendant stood his ground. "Sir, he just wants to see you. Forgive me, but I believe this is a visit you must take."

Arun was already tired and since the last case, he had to give the judgment to evict someone. It made him mentally and physically tired thinking of the people affected by the eviction.

At any rate, despite his earlier reservations about entertaining visitors, curiosity got the better of Arun as he picked up the newspaper.

There was the article, with the headline "Taxi Driver to Judge." He realized that while no one from the newspaper interviewed him, the reporter got hold of other sources close to Arun for the details of his career journey from being a taxi driver to a judge. As he read the article, he recollected those past events as if they had happened yesterday. Arun vaguely remembered some of his family members and friends mentioning to him about being approached by a newspaper writer about an article on his life.

Memories kept flooding back—the time he just got married and was looking for jobs. His new wife Sikhrini was working at the Accountant General of Bengal (AGB) office, a position she got through her older sister Bina, who was one of the chief accountants.

Arun recalled starting each day searching for jobs early in the morning going from office to office looking at postings on the board of various places to check for openings.

As a result of being imprisoned for years at a time due to his fight against British rule, Arun had no job experience. He finished his undergraduate degree in prison, then just before independence, he volunteered at the Peace Camp in East Bengal during the communal riot between Hindus and Muslims. By the time Arun returned from Peace Camp, India gained independence from the British in 1947, but India was divided and became India and Pakistan.

In 1948, Arun managed to get a part time job as co-editor at a popular literary magazine. By August of that year, he married the love of his life, Sikhrini. It was a long awaited event for Sikhrini, who had longed to be Arun's wife since she was in college.

The couple started their life together full of hope and dreams.

They both decided to apply for law school and both were fortunate to be admitted. But they had to work to survive so they took evening classes in order to work in the daytime and as a result, it took them longer to finish law school.

As Arun's job search continued, he faced difficulty in finding a suitable position. While he landed some interviews, they were poorly-paid clerical jobs. Arun was facing a nagging dilemma, whether to accept this kind of job or not, when he met Arjun Singh, who was driving a luxury cab for a living and wanted to complete his masters in Economics in Calcutta University. Inspired by Arjun's determination, Arun learned his line of work and sought Arjun's advice to buy a luxury cab on loan and drive it as his own car while he paid off the loan in installments.

He warned Arun that it would be boring and tiring—night driving jobs at times could be risky with drunken passengers—but Arun was not to be deterred. Arjun Singh suggested that Arun could get a loan easily from the newly-formed Indian government, as he was a political sufferer who fought against the British in the struggle for India's independence.

Arjun Singh and Arun bonded as friends as they met in a coffee house near the University of Calcutta in central Calcutta. As they discussed future plans, Arjun Singh told Arun that he would relieve him of his shift whenever he wanted to take time off. He also suggested that Arun should work independently and run his own cab business, otherwise he would lose money.

The idea of driving a cab for a living was news that Arun's and Sikhrini's family did not take very well. Their families thought that Arun was making a big mistake and bringing shame to the family by taking such a lowly job.

Arun's elder brothers also did not approve as they were concerned about Arun's health and safety at night. They feared he might get robbed and hurt by drunken drivers. His wife, Sikhrini, was also concerned about Arun's safety and health.

Sikhrini's family was vocal about their disapproval. They couldn't fathom that their beloved daughter could ever be married to a man who worked as a taxi driver, a station in life so far beneath them.

But Arun didn't care what anyone thought. He got a loan *and* a highly-coveted sea-green Desoto sedan.

Even today, Arun remembered fondly how after he got the car, he drove with Sikhrini on a long stretch of road called the Grand Trunk Road which was first built by a Moghal Emperor and which stretched all the way to Delhi.

It was twilight of the evening, the oblong moon was just peeping through the branches of Banyan trees and the sky through the avenue of trees which sparkled slowly with a veil of gazing stars. The forward motion of the car, along with the forward force of time, all merged in one that evening.

Arun glanced at his beloved wife. "It is a beautiful evening. I feel the motion of time. It seems it is pulling us to somewhere where there is light."

"I feel this moment should never end, it should stay forever. Imagine if this road never ended and time would stand still. Tell me, is this how you feel?" Sikhrini asked, a twinkle in her eye.

"Sikha, life needs contrast, that is the beauty of life," Arun replied.

Arun and Sikhrini felt a sense that they were about to open a door to the unknown. But they knew that what lay ahead would somehow be magical and attained through their hard work and love.

The blast of evening breeze blew through the car window, tossing Sikhrini's tendrils of long black hair as Arun's deep-set eyes filled with love gazed at her with longing. He touched her thigh softly.

�

Driving a luxury cab for a living included working from morning until late night. Some nights the party goers were drunk and rowdy. He remembered one time his life was threatened as he demanded that the inebriated party goers pay him the correct amount.

Juggling his academic life with his marriage proved to be just as challenging; sometimes he was too tired to stay awake at evening. There was hardly any time to spend with his wife, except attend classes at the law school together. Socially, they were deprived from visits to their friends as Sikhrini did not like how the others would look at Arun when they would learn that Arun was earning his living driving a cab. Arun's confident expression eased Sikhrini's tension most of the time. They both pulled through tough times by encouraging each other and no shortage of hand holding.

⚜⚜⚜

By the end of four years, they graduated from law school and immediately Sikhrini started her position as an advocate at Calcutta High Court as Arun took the competitive civil service exam in law to become a judge as he wanted a steady position in law.

And, the rest, as they say, is all history. A sudden soft knock at the door transported Arun back to the present. His attendant poked his head through the door's crack.

"Sir, may I finally present the gentleman representing the Taxi Drivers Association who is very eager to meet with you?"

Arun nodded. "Please let him in."

III.
Not Just an Ordinary Cab Driver

❧

For Arun, early mornings in 1950 were spent washing his sea-green Desoto cab in front of his apartment building on the street in Bipin Pal Road in the south part of Calcutta.

Then, as he waxed his car, he'd look at it and whisper, "You look happy," as if his car was his beloved girl, and indeed, she was his pride and joy. Arun would look after his car the way other young men and eager car enthusiasts regarded theirs—with the same care.

But of course, his wife, Sikhrini had always been the love of his life and after the daily car cleaning ritual, he would go upstairs in their home to bid his wife goodbye before heading off to work.

Once in his car, he'd cruise along the back roads of his locality and park his car at a taxi stand in a place called Lake Market, a shopping center that was easily accessible for customers interested in hailing a cab.

There was a thatched roadside café at the stand where the taxi drivers usually stopped for their morning tea. The tea was made especially in this cafe, where the milk would be boiled for some time then the tea leaves added and boiled again. When the tea maker would see that the color was just right, he would strain and serve the tea in a glass. Fresh baked round buns went with the tea. It was indeed a special treat.

Arun loved to talk with his fellow drivers while sitting on a roadside bench enjoying his favorite bun and a glass of tea. After finishing his morning tea, he would wait in his cab for passengers.

Some days, he would be hired to go to Howrah station, a main train station on the other side of Ganges. The passengers were headed for their vacation to other states and were very excited to talk about their trip to Arun. A cab driver hanging out at the big train station meant there was always a chance of getting hired soon as so many people would be returning from other states to go to different areas of the city.

The passengers who would hire a taxi where there to visit loved ones at hospitals, often asking the same question as to how much time it would take to reach the hospital.

Arun would politely answer, "I will try my best to take you there as soon as possible." *Didn't people know being a taxi driver meant a tremendous responsibility to one's safety?* Arun thought.

Arun's taxi was often hired to pick up VIPs at the airport as his sea-green cab always used to stand out compared to others.

One time somebody hired him to pick up a VIP from airport. As Arun waited outside, the person who hired him went inside the airport to greet the VIP arrival—the secretary of the department of agriculture. As soon as the passenger boarded the taxi Arun recognized Barun, who was in prison at the same time Arun was.

Barun recognized Arun and after a short conversation came to know that Arun was driving a taxi for a living while he and his wife were studying law together. Barun mentioned to Arun that he would like to share his incredible story of survival if Arun would give him permission to tell his story of how bravely and enthusiastically he was fighting all the odds to make a decent and honest living.

Arun expressed that he was honored by the gesture and when he returned home, he felt joy in his heart at having been validated as someone just trying to do the right thing.

Rainy season in Calcutta—from May through the first week of August—was also wedding season. Heat and humidity would befall the public as the sky would be covered with black clouds, an effect that would soften the landscape.

At intervals, thunder would roll its chariot and lash its lightening, the clattering sound of heavy drops of rain would lull the city in a dreamy mood. In each corner of the shopping center were buckets full of white long-stemmed tuberoses dipped in water and fresh jasmine garlands of different sizes displayed for sale. The tuberoses were sold as a bunch and jasmine garlands were for adorning the neck, the wrist or the hair on one's head.

One of the more interesting experiences was the time Arun's cab was hired for a wedding party. He worked an entire evening shift one time in early August, 1951. Arun's cab client wanted his cab to be decorated with garlands and drive the groom to the bride's place. Arun was worried that his cab might get scratched by the wire used to string the floral decorations together. When the day of the wedding arrived, Arun went to pick the groom up and saw the place was dazzling with lights and flower decorations. There was a colorful tent with chandeliers hanging inside decorated with fresh garlands made of jasmine and roses.

A special space decorated upstairs on the front balcony for musicians called *Nahabat Khana* (*Nahabat,* meaning an assortment of many musical instruments played; *Khana,* meaning place), located in the northern part of India where the *Shenai,* a musical instrument is usually played at the wedding. The musical instrument is thought to have developed by improving upon the *pungi,* a folk instrument used for snake charming. The word *sur* means tone or tune. The word *nai/nali* means reed or pipe. It is a woodwind, with a double reed and metal or wooden flared bell at the other end. Its sound is thought to create and maintain a sense of auspiciousness and sanctity and as a result it is widely used during weddings, processions and in temples.

Arun was relieved to find that professionals decorated his cab with ornate flower garlands, strung with cotton threads.

The time arrived when the groom was ready to board the cab. Dressed in an off-white silk embroidered top with gold buttons, a flowing gold-bordered material wrapped and tied neatly from the waist down, the groom was a sight to behold. A garland made with jasmine and roses with silver sequins at intervals was hanging proudly around his neck. He was crowned with a white conical head gear made of *shola,* crafted carefully with an artistic design called *Topor* in Bengali. The raw material of *shola* was made from the soft stem of a wild-growing water plant.

As soon as the groom boarded the cab, the *shenai* started playing the music at full volume. The female relatives who were adorned in their beautiful saris and jewelry started blowing the conch shells as the mother of the groom placed her hand on the head of the groom to bless him and then the cab started its journey to the bride's place.

When the cab arrived at the bride's residence, where the wedding would take place, the house was illuminated with lights and was dazzling with more unique decor.

Shenai at the bride's place was full blast as the elegantly-dressed ladies arrived with their conch shells and showered the groom with rose petals.

The mother-in-law-to-be dressed in a red-bordered sari with a large vermillion *bindi* in the middle of her forehead came out with a sandalwood paste in a small silver bowl to welcome the groom.

Arun had to go back and fetch those who were left behind at the groom's place before returning to the bride's residence where he would wait in case anyone else needed a ride.

Arun came with a load of groom's relatives to the bride's place. As he tried to take a break, members of the wedding party requested him to join them for dinner but he politely refused, preferring to wait in his cab. And while he sat inside the cab, Arun started reminiscing about his own wedding.

❀❀❀

The day in August 1948 when Arun made the beautiful Sikhrini his wife, it was also cloudy—raining off and on. As a cool breeze was blowing slowly, the moon struggled to emerge through the black clouds and there was a glow over the horizon.

The rain and breeze washed tree branches causing them to sway gently, their round blossoms emanating an effervescent scent in the air.

Arun remembered the day he came out from his elder brother's house dressed in his groom's attire, a garland of jasmine and roses around his neck. He missed his mother who passed away a year prior. She would've been the one blessing her son before the wedding.

Held at 114 Monohor Pukur Road in South Calcutta, the wedding location was very close to where he lived now, Arun noted. His wedding day was one of the most exciting and happiest days of his life. It was hard to believe that just a few weeks before their wedding day, Sikhrini's parents finally agreed to the couple's union after much resistance.

Arun recalled seeing Sikhrini's mother sigh as her shoulders slumped when he arrived at their home with his proposal of marriage. Even as Arun was working part-time as an editor in a literary journal, Sikhrini's mother claimed that Arun could not even provide cosmetics for her daughter.

With the intervention of Sikhrini's two elder sisters, Sikhrini's parents agreed to the marriage. On the evening of the wedding, Arun arrived at his bride's residence where he was surprised to be warmly greeted by Sikhrini's very attractive mother.

Scenes of Arun's wedding kept on flashing in his mind, especially the image of his beautiful bride dressed in a special red sari with gold jewelry accents as she circled around him seven times. After the seventh time, the bride and groom stood face-to-face exchanging a loving gaze as if they were looking at each other for the first time. As a red veil draped over his bride's head, Arun remembered how beautiful she looked and that he could not take his eyes off her.

The couple took their vows in front of fire made by the priest with a special kind of wood. As the fire rose to greater heights, the priest uttered the Sanskrit word, *Slokas* or hymn, which the couple repeated then prayed to *Agni*, the god of fire and *Swaha*, his wife.

At the end, the couple circled the fire and took seven steps. The bride was in front and moved forward with Arun, her life partner, to take the steps of married life. Then Arun remembered the priest who took Arun's right hand and placed Sikhrini's right palm on her new husband's palm. They sat face to face as they offered prayers with a jasmine garland binding their palms together. This was a romantic and sensuous moment that Arun would never forget.

Arun had planned a perfect honeymoon night, preparing roses and jasmine for Sikhrini. After taking a shower, Arun sprayed his favorite *attar*, or cologne, and scattered the fresh jasmine all over the marital bed, keeping a bunch of roses on Sikhrini's bedside table.

He rehearsed his suggestion to his new bride: "Tomorrow, we will ride in a small boat in the Ganges and sit side-by-side, hand-in-hand. We'll share lunch with the boatman as we watch the beauty of the Ganges and join the chorus with the boatman singing an old river song."

Just as he wished, Sikhrini agreed to his plan as he gently crawled in bed with her and immediately they embraced tightly. Outside, the moonlight peeped through the window as frogs croaked and crickets started their serenade.

Cheers from the wedding guests he chauffeured awakened Arun from reminiscing about his own wedding. He would go on to drive the taxi cab to continue to make ends meet.

Four long years later, Sikhrini and Arun got their law degrees. Sikhrini began her law practice with the Calcutta high court as Arun passed the test of Indian civil service exam in law and started working as a small court judge in Barasat a district town, close to Calcutta.

They lived a topsy-turvy life—Arun started a steady job but had to commute back and forth, while Sikhrini had to start from scratch in her new profession.

They lived simply at their cozy apartment, thinking the place was tailor-made for them as a haven to rest, to talk, to laugh, and share their feelings about life which were sometimes sad and sometimes joyous. Here they slept cozily together and dreamt that life would always be as sweet as it was as long as they were together.

And then there was the cab, the beautiful sea-green cab, they had to eventually part with. Every morning Arun would take care of the cab, wash and wax it. Like a child he would take care of it, but now the time had come for him and the trusty sea-green cab to go their separate ways.

So Arun and Sikhrini thanked the sea-green cab's contribution to making their lives smoother as they were able to pay off the loan they took from the government.

Their cab was sold to a friend of theirs named Katrick who had a taxi cab business and assured Sikhrini and Arun that their cab would be in good hands.

"I will use it as my personal car," Katrick said.

Arun and Sikhrini were relieved for that beloved sea-green cab had helped them earn a decent living. Now, it was time to move on. For the last time they took a ride on their sea-green cab to Katrick's house.

They were happy to see the cab had a nicely-covered stall and someone who would take care of the car. And just as the sea-green car had embraced a new life, so would Arun and Sikhrini welcome a new and brighter future ahead.

IV.
Majer Ganthi

৵

Arun took off his black judge's robe in his chamber at the Alipore courthouse and sighed. Going down memory lane was heartwarming but now he had to focus on the present—the life he worked so hard to build.

While on a luncheon recess, he was looking forward to relaxing—that is, until his attendant came in and asked him what he would like to eat. Arun replied with his usual request.

"Sir, I would like to leave early as the roads will be blocked caused by a huge rally," the attendant said. "The Calcutta Chemical workers are demanding higher wages."

Arun nodded. He was aware that year, in 1960, Calcutta Chemical workers were not being paid adequate wages commensurate with their efforts and the rising cost of living.

"It is all right," Arun replied, solemnly. "You can leave early."

৵৵৵

Arun remembered years ago during a break from his second year of college, when he went back to his home in Majer Ganthi, a cozy town in the district of the state of Khulna, located in East Pakistan.

In 1940, Arun was only nineteen, sporting shiny black hair and brown skin, standing slim at five-feet-ten inches tall. His spirited charm and confidence fascinated those around him. Standing tall with his aquiline nose, bright black eyes, slick ebony hair and penchant for conversation, Arun would command attention in every room.

Mainly known as agricultural town, Majer Ganthi had acres of land where residents there owned paddy fields to grow their own rice and maintain fruit orchards of their own all year round. The house his family lived in was surrounded by small orchards of mango, jackfruit and litchi trees. There was also a medium-sized pond, with coconut and palm trees that lined the boundaries of their property. A substantial vegetable garden and paddy fields of rice also adorned their property. For Arun, who came from a middle class family, there was just the sufficient amount of resources for eight children and the parents. They learned to live off their own land with the idealism of "simple living and high thinking." The family prioritized education to ensure a bright future for the children.

During this time, Savitri, Arun's mother, who was a widow in her mid-fifties, looked very attractive with streaks of gray accenting her long black hair. Her sari, which would be either green or blue, bordered with a white sari tucked neatly with a matching blouse. Her tanned skin and triangular face with beautiful big black eyes made her a standout in the crowd. After morning prayers, she would apply a *bindi* of sandalwood paste on the middle of her forehead.

Her husband, who died a few years prior, was in the civil service, so Arun's mother received a pension from her husband's employer. His father left some money in the bank for his wife so Arun's mother was able to access money from her late husband's life insurance to ensure she and her children could remain in the family home where she raised her children.

One time when Arun went back to visit his mother, she seemed to be preoccupied and her facial expression showed anxiety and concern.

She was breathing heavily and repeated some words more than once and often sighing. It was obvious when she started talking that her anxiety was caused by Arun's activities and she asked several questions regarding Arun's whereabouts and plans.

As one of her eight children, Arun was second to the youngest. The older children were grown and living their own lives in different parts of India. Two of them were based in Calcutta.

Surprised to see his mother so agitated, Arun admitted to being involved with an organization named Forward Bloc, a revolutionary group fighting against British. This was in 1940 and India was under British domination. Younger generations of Indian citizens, under the leadership of their elders were all preparing to strike back against the British, however they could.

They tried to paralyze the domination led by the revolutionary leader, Subhas Chandra Bose, a highly-educated, resourceful man who sought the help of young enthusiastic college students. Arun was among them.

While Bose's ideology and philosophy did not match with Mahatma Gandhi's, his vision was aligned with any other nationalistic hero. Bose was known for his political acumen and military knowledge. He founded the Azad Hind Fauj—the Indian National Army—and as commander-in-chief, he was known to the public as *Netaji*. Under British prime minister Clement Atlee, India gained independence in 1947. Atlee claimed that it was Bose who led the Indian National Army that weakened the very foundation of British troops and inspired the Royal Navy mutiny in 1946, leading the British to believe that they no longer were in a position to rule India.

Somehow Arun's mother, Savitri, came to know about her son's revolutionary involvement a month prior from her friend whose husband was also involved in Forward Bloc. She had obtained information that the young followers would gather in Calcutta *Maidan*, an open space for gathering and public speaking. From there, the gathering would march to a secretarial building, called Writer's Building.

Savitri knew all about Netaji, who was a great orator and would impress and inspire the young men with his battle cry: "Give me blood and I will give you freedom."

"Arun, are you going to *Maidan* and march to Writer's Building?"

Arun answered solemnly, "Yes, Mother."

"Will you be carrying secret plans and documents from Subhas Chandra—the document which explains the future line of action of the Forward Bloc Party and new tactics to assault the British Government?"

With his eyes blinking rapidly, Arun was slightly shocked with how much information his mother knew. "Yes, Mother."

"You should have a companion nearby if anything were to happen to you," she paused, breathing heavily. "If you are arrested or injured, he can vouch for you."

Puzzled and slightly repulsed, Arun asked, "Why you are thinking like that?"

"Arun, I fear that something terrible is going to happen to you!"

"Mother!" He was annoyed by her negative prophetic comment.

"Yes, Arun," his mother replied anxiously. "I'm afraid you will be arrested and I do not want to think the worse, but still, I fear there will be tear gas, and mounted police will charge and, God forbid, who knows, they might charge their guns. And, and . . ."

"Mother! Please. There's nothing to fear. This is an important mission that must be undertaken if we as a people can be free."

His mother pouted. "Yes, mothers are always worried about their children."

Arun's expression softened. "Are you trying to say I should not go?"

Savitri looked at him sternly. "Arun you are wrong. I am not the kind of person to tell you what to do when you are in the freedom fight for India. I just have this premonition. I see things."

As she started spinning the wheel, a crow started cawing outside and a train whistled by.

കകക

As planned, everyone gathered in the *Maidan*, a big open space for public gathering and speaking, as Subhas Chandra Bose started his speech, a person handed Arun a bundle of papers.

"Please keep this and give it to the other leader, Hemen Bose as soon as possible," the man told Arun. "Netaji is leaving the country shortly and these are his secret plans to be carried out by the Forward Bloc Party."

After the speech, people began marching. Shouts of "British leave India! *Bande mataram* and Glory to our Mother!" filled the air.

Suddenly amid a big blast of tear gas, the mounted police charged at the group and gunshots were heard. Arun saw Ganendra, a twelve-year-old boy, braving the march.

"Please take these papers and run," Arun pleaded with the boy. "These are secret plans of Subhas Bose.

Make sure you hand it over to the other nationalist Hemen Bose."

The young boy grabbed the papers and hid them under his shirt. Taking off, he ran as fast as he could as Arun saw him arrive safely on the other side of *Maidan*.

As police started beating protesters, Arun was one of those caught, beaten and later arrested and locked up in Alipore prison. In his cell, Arun buried his face in his hands. *Mother's premonitions proved to be correct.*

That solemn memory was enough to snap Arun back to the present where he was filled with gratitude that he and his family were safe, sound and free.

"It seems that life has come full circle," thought Arun as he looked around the judge's chamber where he had sat musing about the past.

❦❦❦

A quiet knock at the door signaled the arrival of the attendant with Arun's lunch.

"Sir, I did not ask what you want to drink—tea, coffee or *lassi*."

"Tea is fine."

The Alipore courthouse was very close to Alipore prison. While commuting to work in the morning, Arun's eyes glanced at the red brick building and while heading home, he would gaze at the light and shadows that cast on the bricks of Alipore prison. It wasn't difficult to flash back to the memories of the small cell where he was imprisoned.

Arun, looked around the room, and murmured quietly to himself. "Destiny."

V.
Chasing the End to Begin Anew

❧

At the courthouse in Calcutta, the building was quieter as few people were working late, Arun being one of them. Today was a special day for Arun—his three-year-old grandson was visiting him at the courthouse.

The little boy, named Dibya, with his big black sparkling eyes, had an endless curiosity and limitless energy. He looked taller for a three-year-old, with a healthy body, round face, thick black hair, and lightly-tanned skin. When he smiled, a dimple appeared on his right cheek. A very happy little fellow, he was either singing to himself or talking nonstop or bombarding lots of questions to the attendant.

The boy was fascinated to see the old court room with its mahogany wooden benches which were arranged in a semicircular manner. There was an upper level stage-like structure. In the middle sat a heavy wooden round-shaped padded swivel chair. In front of this chair stood a polished wooden table. On one side of this stage there was a raised desk and by its side a few wooden steps descended down to the lower level.

On the back side of the stage another set of wooden steps went down to a room where his Grandfather was working at present. Dibya noticed that there were a few ceiling fans and pointed at them excitedly.

A long, thick, red-frilled broad cloth hung from one end of the room to the other and was draped just above the heavy chair and the desk. This also captured Dibya's attention as he exclaimed, "What's that?"

The attendant explained in olden days there was no electric fans so two people used to pull this heavy cloth with ropes tied to either side for air to circulate during hot weather. The people who used to operate them were called *pankhawalla*.

The attendant tried to explain his Grandfather Arun's work to the little boy as he showed Dibya the chair and explained that his Grandfather would sit and listen to the case trials and give judgment.

Dibya nodded and seemed to understand. "I want to sit on my *Dadu's* chair," said the excited little boy, referring to Arun by his pet name for "Grandpa."

The attendant picked him up and placed him on the chair. Dibya started singing and swirling around in the chair.

Arun witnessed his grandson's excitement from his room where he was working, pleased that his Dibya was happy and sitting in his chair. The old smell of this courtroom reminded him of the past when he became a lower court judge for the first time. That was when his daughter, Rita, the mother of Dibya, was born thirty years ago in 1954.

The past events kept on flashing in his mind like a movie screen.

He remembered engaging in oil painting, one of his hobbies. He did some oil painting while he was in prison where he somehow managed to get art materials with the warden's permission. While imprisoned, he was also allowed to complete his undergraduate degree.

After he was released from prison, Arun got involved in a door-to-door campaign to collect money for a political organization he was involved with. This was to be an auspicious and unforgettable day.

One of the houses he approached happened to be where Sikhrini was living. He could see from the open screened door his future wife who was eighteen years old at the time as she came rushing down the stairs to greet him. Her long black hair was tied up in a bun. She was about five-feet-four inches tall with lightly-tanned skin. Her heart-shaped face framed a slender nose and beautiful big black eyes. Sikhrini frowned at him and her eyes glittered with frustration.

But she wasn't rushing to greet him after all. "I am late for my class."

Already smitten, Arun asked for an apology and said, "I will come back later."

Arun instantly fell in love with Sikhrini. He went back to his childhood home where he painted Sikhrini standing under a tree, looking at a flowing river where small boats were sailing.

As promised, Arun returned to Sikhrini's home, ostensibly to gather monetary donations and while there, he came to know Sikhrini's two elder sisters. The oldest sister was married but Sikhrini and Bina both were college students at the time, living with their older sister.

Slowly but very surely Sikhrini became very much attracted to the charming Arun. They would meet at a café after Sikhrini's college classes and talk. Whenever Arun would finish a painting he would present it to Sikhrini who would award him with a look of gratitude in her luminous eyes.

They would walk on the promenade along the Ganges river to watch the sunset and ride a boat, a cool breeze caressing their flushed cheeks.

Dibya's piercing laughter brought Arun back to the present. At sixty-three years old, he still stood tall with touches of gray hair on the either side of his forehead. Despite the creased lines on his weathered face, there was still a hint of his boyish charm in the mature man he evolved into.

While he longed to retire three years' prior from his judiciary career, he felt forced to continue working after taking a leave of absence to go to London to obtain credential as a bonafide officer of the court of law. While this opportunity was very prestigious, Sikhrini pointed out to him, it was not necessary. It would be just another title, Arun's wife asserted, and he didn't need to prove his worth by passing the bar exam in London.

After being mired in a dilemma between experiencing the adventure of living in London versus staying at home, Arun ultimately decided to go to London, with his wife's support, taking a leave of absence from work.

It was decided that Sikhrini would stay at home with their children and continue to practice as an advocate in Calcutta high court. It was a very hard decision, but they both thought that was the right thing to do.

So Arun sailed to England. Besides the constant cold and rain, he had to work hard there to survive and pay the tuition for the course and exorbitant fees to study and pass the bar examination. Once again, despite his education, Arun proved that no job was beneath him as he worked as a waiter and helped out in the campus kitchen of the university, as well as worked as an assistant to a motor mechanic.

All his hard work and studying paid off. Arun cruised through the tough bar exam in only his first attempt at it in 1964.

Was it worth it? Arun asked himself. He got his answer. Yes. Before his London trip, his career had become dormant and he didn't want to be stereotyped as a typical attorney who took the fast track to becoming a judge. While his London experience proved to be a challenge. He was proud he completed it. It shaped him to be a better, much stronger person in a much different manner than the time he was involved in the fight against the British. Even the time he spent in prison and when he was beaten badly by police during the British regime in India had made him stronger in mind, body and spirit. Despite fighting against the British, Arun's decision to study in London was sort of a personal dare to himself that he could indeed survive in the harsh and inclement weather and grueling bar examination offered by the country that had once ruled his home. And from a compassionate and forgiving standpoint, his stay in London was his way of making peace with the British— for when one stops to think about it, had it not been for the British occupation, Arun wouldn't have become the strong man he was today.

As he thought about the challenges he overcame, Arun understood that the "the feeling and yearning burns you inside which could move you forward or make you exhausted. The fire which burns inside you could make you a better person; with its light one can see the image of self and purify oneself to become a better human being."

He also paused to honor his beloved wife, Sikhrini, who had been with him through it all the joys and trials and sacrifices. *She did not fail to stand or leave me*, he thought. *Her love is like an eternal fire.*

Arun regarded Sikhrini now, as an eternally-beautiful fifty-eight-year-old woman, wife, established lawyer and Grandmother, who still had the same enthusiasm about life and love ever since the day they met. Even streaks of gray hair blended into her ebony cascades hadn't diminished the spirit of the woman he fell for all those years ago.

After his return from London, for old times sake, Arun invited Sikhrini for a promenade along the Ganges to enjoy the sunset. Time outside the city of Calcutta for a short vacation was just what the couple needed as they reminisced while strolling and driving around the area surrounded by mountains and tall trees full of red blossoms in spring and green meadows etched with colorful wildflowers. They would spend time there sitting along a roadside thatched café watching the passersby and gazing at the mountains with their bluish hue.

He was startled by Dibya's voice. "*Dadu*, I want to go home, I miss *Didam* and Ma," said the little boy referring to Sikhrini and his mother, Arun's daughter.

"You are right. Dadu's already put in a long work day and now it's time to go and enjoy the day with our family," Arun said, patting his grandson's head. "I am glad you came to visit me here. Do you remember the song that I taught you the other day?"

Dibya nodded eager as he clapped his hands and started singing happily the lyrics from *Taser Desh*, an epic about freedom composed by the great poet Rabindranath Tagore:

Amra Sabai Raja, Amaderi Rajar Rajatta
Amra Sabai Raja . . .

And as Arun's baritone voice blended with his grandson's high-pitched vocals, a tear of love and gratitude rolled down his cheek.

Acknowledgments

Janice De Jesus is my creative writing guru and my special young friend who inspired me to embark on writing my own collection of short stories.

When I joined her class few years ago, I did not exactly know what 'creative writing' meant. Her inspiration and guidance showed me the path to fulfill my desire to write down my stories.

Most of my stories blossomed either from her prompts, or from her casual conversation. I cannot thank her enough, but realize deeply that she showed me the realm of a vast horizon yet to be discovered.

I thank Karen Mireau for the enormous job she did in the process of publishing this book. Her artwork, editing, networking and her constant encouragement and inspiration were invaluable.

Lastly and not least I thank my writing group—they are special friends and my extended family.

About the Author

Poet and short story writer Maya Mitra Das was born in India and came to the U.S. in 1973. She studied internal medicine and pediatrics in India, England and the United States, earning her M.D. and Ph.D. She received her training at Downstate Medical Center and State University Hospital in Brooklyn, New York.

She completed two fellowships—one for the Department of Hematology and Oncology at U.C.L.A. Medical Center and the second at the University of California, San Francisco, for radiation oncology. She currently serves on the medical staff at Children's Hospital in Oakland, California.

Among her many interests and hobbies, Maya performs 'Bharatnatyam' Indian classical dance. Her poetry has appeared in *Tuesday's Poetry*, edited by Jerry Ball, and two narrative poems have been anthologized in *What's in a Name*, edited by Elaine Starkman. Her fiction has previously appeared in *Tremors: Short Fiction by California Writers*.

*This collection of short stories by Maya Mitra Das
may be ordered directly at www.lulu.com.*

*For events or more information,
please visit http://silhouettesoftime.blogspot.com*

*To schedule an interview or signing with the author, please contact
the publisher at:*

Azalea.Art.Press@gmail.com / 510.919.6117
or visit http://azaleaartpress.blogspot.com